Deacon Brown's Daughters

by

CaSandra McLaughlin & Michelle Stimpson

ISBN: 1-943563-08-X

Published by MLStimpson Enterprises
P.O. Box 1592
Cedar Hill, TX 75106
United States of America

Editing by Michelle Chester, www.ebm-services.com

Dedication

For my daddy, J.D. Marshall. Thanks for all you do for me.
Love you!
-CaSandra McLaughlin

For Kalise. I pray that you will know God as the best Father ever!
-Michelle Stimpson

Acknowledgments

Michelle & Cassie want to thank God for the gift of writing. We give Him all the glory and honor for the things He allows us to do. It's always our goal to keep Him the main focus in all we do.

Thanks to all the fans and followers who continue to spread the word, too. We love you!

CHAPTER 1

He was used to getting messages from random women. These days, the messages usually came through his phone in the form of a text or an email. Whoever wrote this one must have had a lot on her mind because she had taken the time and effort to write neat, cursive letters on the front and use an oversized envelope.

It was addressed To: Stanley David Brown, Care of: Effie Brown, followed by his mother's address in Big Oak, TX.

Stanley chuckled to himself as he laid the envelope on his nightstand. Whatever this blast from the past had to say to him would have to wait until he got out of his work clothes and had a glass of Jack Daniels to warm up.

No. Not Jack Daniels. He had to remind himself that he was a changed man. Even a whole year after accepting Christ, his mind returned to its old default ways without conscious resistance. Though Stanley had never been an alcoholic, he recognized alcohol as a gateway to the past for him. No need in going back there.

Besides, it was two in the afternoon. Saturday overtime was always finished before he knew it. Coffee was still in order.

"Stan-laaaaay!"

He ignored his mother. She would call at least three more times before adding his middle and last name.

Stanley slid his aching feet from the steel-toed boots he'd purchased for his new job as a forklift operator. The position was well below his intelligence, but probably right in line with what his work history was worth. He was one of the oldest men working

1

in that position at Transit Systems Deluxe. Most of the men his age didn't work the dock. They were truck drivers, dispatchers, supervisors. Too old to be outside in the cold trying to coerce 52-year-old bones to keep pushing.

The tender spots on his feet welcomed the soft carpet as he walked down the short hall between his current bedroom and the bathroom.

"Stan-laaaaay!"

That was only twice. He knew he should respond to her, but he also knew what she wanted, and he couldn't give her an answer yet to who had written him a letter and mailed it without a return address. Out of respect, he yelled, "Wait a minute, Momma," as he shut the door behind him.

The two-story home had been one of the most well-kept homes on their street when he was a little boy. But his mother had refused to update the house. She replaced things as they were needed, but hadn't put any real effort into replacing the linoleum tile or removing the flowered wallpaper. "Keeps the character," she had said.

Now that Stanley was home, he'd offered to at least paint over the wallpaper. He'd seen it done once on a do-it-yourself show.

"Naw, leave it be. It'll be back in style in a little while," Effie refused.

If somebody had told Stanley a year ago, before he went to that Sunday morning service at Lee Chapel, that he'd be moving back home to take care of his mother, he would have told them they'd been drinking too much.

Stanley ran his hand along his chin. He could have used a good shave. He'd have to shave, actually, before Sunday night. Part of the work dress code.

He turned his head to the left. To the right. Admiring his profile in the bathroom mirror. He smiled at his reflection—smooth, deep-brown skin, white teeth, a broad nose, and grayish-green eyes that caused even the most modest woman to do a double-take. At which point, he always blinked and flashed all 32. That's all it took, for the most part. Then came a date or two. Maybe three if his game wasn't slippin'. Then came the bedroom and she'd be all his after that.

If he couldn't get anything else, he could always get a woman. And with a woman came food, a place to stay, and electricity. That's all he'd ever needed to survive.

Until Jesus.

He straightened up tall and stuck his chest out, still admiring his 6'4" frame. Those guys on the dock might have been younger and faster, but none of them would look half as good as him at his age.

Stanley turned on the shower to let the water warm up.

An old house like this still needed time to do what it was supposed to do. Kind of like his feet and back, which had not yet decided that they were on the work-six-days-a-week plan.

"Stanley David Brown!"

Time was up.

Stanley briskly walked to the kitchen and stood over his mother. This woman right here could work his nerves something fierce. "Momma, stop hollering my name. I'm right in the next room."

"You actin' like you can't hear me, though!" She folded her newspaper and looked up at him over the rim of her glasses. Stanley saw the gray ring around her eyes, the wrinkles circling her neck, even the knobs on her knuckles from arthritis. His sister, Emily, had been right. Momma couldn't have moved to Detroit with them for Emily's husband's new job. The trip would have taken a toll on her body, not to mention the fit she would have thrown about leaving her house.

In an instant, Stanley was thankful to have been in a position to step in where Emily had to leave off.

Effie motioned toward Stanley's bedroom. "Who that letter

from?"

"I don't know yet."

"One of your women?"

"I don't have any women."

"Hmph. That's a first."

Stanley shook his head. "I'm going to take a shower now."

"Well, bring the letter to me. I'll open it."

"No can do. It's addressed to me. If you open it, that's a felony."

"Felony my foot. Long as you stayin' under my roof, I got rights! I shoulda opened it already, anyway, since it came to my care. Now, come on and open it else I'll sneak in there and open it while you in the shower."

Stanley laughed. "If you tell me you're going to sneak, that's not actually sneaking, now is it?"

Effie slapped his arm. "You stop it. Go on. Turn off that shower water and come back in here."

"I don't smell good," Stanley teased.

"You smell like a hard-working man, and that's the best smell ever. Now, stop playin' with me and get the letter before you make me have a heart attack from worryin'."

Drama.

Stanley dutifully obeyed. He turned off the water, grabbed the letter, and joined his mother at the kitchen table again. The table wobbled a bit, which meant the folded up paper he'd put under the short leg must have wiggled itself loose. Stanley reached down and tucked the paper back in place again. His mother wouldn't dream of letting this table go.

"This is the highlight of your day, huh?" He sulked, tearing the back flap off the envelope while looking into his mother's bucked eyes.

"Might be a late Christmas present. It's only been a week or so."

"Could be," Stanley agreed, though he doubted it. This was probably some woman from his past who wanted to let him know how he'd ruined her life, her credit, her trust in men or in all of humanity. He'd heard it all before: *I thought you were the one! You deserve an Emmy award for your acting skills!*

Truth be told: There was nothing a woman could say to him that he hadn't already beaten himself up about, especially in the past year as he had begun to realize his new identity. He almost wished he could round them all up on a football field, get a bullhorn, and announce to them, "I am sorry. I wish I could change the past, but I can't. I apologize for whatever I might have done to hurt you. Y'all can go on home now."

And then, of course, he would take off running.

"Oh no!" His mother gasped.

Stanley's attention turned to the contents now. He pulled out a folded program. The front of it had a bright yellow sticky note: *F.Y.I.*

He removed the note and came face to face with the picture of a young man who was the spitting image of the face he'd just been adoring in the mirror.

Stanley's heart felt like a stone rock in his chest.

"What is it?" Effie asked.

"An obituary."

Effie's hand covered her neck. "Who?"

"My son."

CHAPTER 2

Remembering the life of Toddderick Jamon Brown. Stanley did the math on his own son's sunrise and sunset dates and arrived at the age of 22. *My son is dead.*

Though Effie was asking questions, Stanley could barely hear her.

He opened the program and read the first two lines of Todderick's life description. *Toddderick was born in Dallas, TX. He was raised in Little Elm, TX by his mother, Rhonda Richardson.*

No mention of Stanley at all.

He jumped down to the last paragraph. *Toddderick is survived by his mother; his sister, Lisa (Mike), and nephew Montez; and a host of uncles, aunts, cousins, and friends.*

Stanley's name was still nowhere on the page.

"What happened to him?" Stanley finally heard his mother say.

"Um..." Stanley stalled. He quickly read through the body of the obituary and found the usual verbiage—accepted Christ at an early age, finished high school, took classes at a community college. He scanned the collage of pictures on the right side of the program to see if he could get a hint about Toddderick's health. All of the photos showed a bright smile, vibrant eyes, and a friendly disposition. There was no sign of Toddderick having suffered a recent illness.

"Doesn't say what happened to him," Stanley answered.

"Gimme the program." Effie all but snatched it out of his hand.

Stanley breathed again. Saw the sticky note again. *F.Y.I. For his* information. How cruel was that? And Rhonda hadn't even put his name in the program. Furthermore, she hadn't even told him that their son was dead until after the funeral.

"She ain't got us nowhere in here," his mother voiced the shameful truth. "Way she wrote this, you'd think she made the boy all by herself. Goodness gracious, Stanley, them last two of your children's momma's is something else! Plum crazy! This kind of foolishness right here is why I couldn't hardly deal with them!"

Stanley stood and walked softly to his bedroom. *My only son is dead.* Though he hadn't seen Todderick more than a few times, somehow this death still struck a violent blow to his entire being. A part of him was gone. The relationship Stanley had hoped they would someday have—whenever Todderick wanted to start it— would never be.

This wasn't right. Rhonda shouldn't have informed him this way. Stanley was Todderick's father, after all. Sending a sticky note on an obituary was low, even for Rhonda.

Without thinking much about what he would say, Stanley called his sister.

"Hey, Stanley."

"Hi. Emily." Words seemed to croak from his throat, as though he was using his vocal chords for the very first time.

"Is everything okay? Momma okay?"

"Yeah. Momma's fine."

Emily sighed. "Good. You okay? You sound like something's wrong."

"Yeah. It is. My son, Todderick. He died."

A gasp came through the phone. "I'm so sorry to hear that. I really wish we had gotten to know him. How old was he? Eighteen? Nineteen?"

"Twenty-two," Stanley corrected her.

"Mmm, mmm, mmm. So young," Emily said in a sympathetic tone. "You going to the funeral?"

Stanley cleared his throat. "They already had it. Rhonda sent me the obituary."

"What? That's crazy? Why didn't she tell you ahead of time? We could have done something to help," Emily said.

That was just like his sister to try to be of assistance, somehow some way.

"I need some help. I lost touch with Rhonda, but you know somebody in her sister's husband's family, right?"

"I don't think her sister is married to Johnny Beuchamp anymore, but I can call one of my classmates and find out. They have a private group online. I'm sure she can help us."

"Thanks."

"Stanley. Are you telling me you've had no contact at all with your son?"

He brisked at her question. There were circumstances surrounding this situation. Circumstances that were none of her business. "No. I'm telling you that I need Rhonda's number."

"Don't get an attitude," Emily quipped.

"I don't want to talk about it."

"Fine. I'll let you know what I find out."

"That'll do. Just text me."

Stanley ended the call before she could ask anything else.

He showered, then returned to his bedroom to find a text with Rhonda's phone number. Emily added a personal note: *I'm sorry if I offended you. I love you, bro.*

Stanley smiled. Emily had a way of making everybody feel loved. He needed to find himself a woman like that one day.

He thought about putting off the call to Rhonda, but wasn't that the reason he was in the predicament now—putting things off? Waiting until the right time to reach out? There probably wouldn't be a "right" time to have closure about Todderick's life and death. Now was as good a time as any.

With jittery fingers, Stanley dialed Rhonda's number.

"Hello?" the deep, scratchy voice he remembered said.

"Hello, Rhonda. It's Stanley."

"Well, look what the cat drug in." She laughed slightly.

"I got the obituary." Stanley didn't know what to say next, so he waited for Rhonda's lead.

"Okay. And?"

"May I ask...what happened?"

"No, you may not."

He'd have to try another angle. "Um...well...was he...sick?"

"I just said I wasn't going to tell you. What part of 'no' didn't you understand?"

"Come on, Rhonda. He was my son, too."

"Really? Your *son*? This boy you hadn't seen since his third birthday party at Pete's Pizza was your *son*?"

Stanley kept his voice at an even keel despite Rhonda's rising pitch. "That was a long time ago."

"It sure was!"

"And you know the circumstances. It wouldn't have been good."

"It *would have been good* for Todderick to have a father. It *would have been good* for him to have a role model. Somebody to look up to. Somebody to call a Dad instead of trying to run with the wrong crowd and fit in with these hoodlums in the neighborhood."

Stanley had heard all he needed to hear. Todderick must have gotten caught up trying to live a wild lifestyle.

"I blame you, Stanley Brown. Todderick wanted to know his father," she screamed.

"He could have called me," Stanley said.

"Why should he have to call you? Why couldn't you call him? You're the adult."

"I didn't have your number," Stanley said.

"But you somehow managed to get it today," she reasoned truthfully.

Busted. Stanley took a deep breath. "Look, I wasn't a good person back then, Rhonda. I was lying to you and the woman I was living with. I was young. Selfish. I should have been there for Todderick, but I wasn't. And I'm sorry."

"I agree. You *are* sorry. You were a sorry, no-good, cheatin', deadbeat father to Todderick and I hate that he's not here to tell you these words himself. But I hope your other kids live to tell you about yourself, and I hope you die alone in the back room of a nasty, stinky government hospital, thinking about all the people you hurt because that is exactly what you deserve."

"Rhon—"

"Lose my number, Stanley. *My* son is dead. There's no reason for us to speak again. Ever."

His phone screen showed "Call Ended."

Stanley didn't remember the drive to church for the Saturday afternoon brotherhood meeting at Warren Grove Missionary Baptist Church. All he knew was that he was sitting right where he needed to be—in church. Where sinners went to repent. Where people tried to make things right.

But I'm not practicing sin anymore.

He had received forgiveness from God for his sins, thanks to Christ. And yet, somehow, the death of the son he never knew made Stanley feel like the devil's best friend. Wrong. All kinds of wrong. And evil. And crazy for ever believing that his past could be erased.

Rhonda's words replayed over and over in his head. *I agree. You are sorry.*

The brotherhood meeting always took place in the fellowship hall because the choir would often practice on Saturdays. It was a mid-sized room. Probably held a hundred people or so at full capacity, but Stanley was glad there weren't too many people at the meeting. He liked the fact that he could ask a question and not feel like he was on display in their quaint setting.

While Brother Aaron Rodgers discussed Hebrews chapter 1, which opened with Scriptures about what God had done for believers through Christ, Stanley found more comfort from the sweet hymns emanating from the sanctuary. Music always calmed him.

In the past, songs like Lenny's "I Love You" and Luther Ingram's "If Loving You is Wrong I Don't Want to be Right" spoke to his soul. The blues and even some country songs hit the spot.

Now, Stanley found solace in songs that reminded him of this new life. He couldn't hear all the words of the song the choir was practicing, but he caught the chorus—He's able.

Those two words, coupled with the focus on Hebrews, built up Stanley's confidence again. He was not the same man who had fathered a child—children, actually—and not really spoken to them over the years. He was a new man. A better man. And there he was on a Saturday sitting in a church house. And he had moved back home to care for his ailing mother. And he'd held a full-time, hard-labor job. He even worked voluntary overtime.

Sorry men didn't do that.

"Brothers, before we close, I want to let you all know that Warren Grove is looking for a few *good* men to join our Deacon's board. We're adding more community outreach services, so the board is expanding. If you're interested in joining these good men, please let me know by next week."

Stanley liked the sound of that. *Good* men. His hand seemed to raise itself.

"Yes, Brother Brown?" Brother Rodgers asked.

Before he could re-think the idea that popped into his head, Stanley said, "I'm interested."

The small gathering of men clapped in recognition of the boldness that Stanley hadn't even realized was in his body.

"Alrighty then. I'll be sure to let Pastor Roundtree know. You'll hear from one of the Deacons soon."

Stanley nodded.

The brotherhood meeting dismissed and a few of the men clapped Stanley on the shoulder, telling him that he was really "coming along" at Warren Grove. But Stanley wasn't worried about Warren Grove. He wanted that feeling. He wanted to know that he was a good man.

Rhonda's scathing rant wasn't any worse than the thoughts he had thought about himself throughout the years. Truth was: Stanley had three more children. Daughters. Yolanda, Kim, and Sabrina. As far as he knew, they were still alive. There was a time to let them meet this new man he was in Christ. He would make them proud, be the kind of father they would be happy to take selfies with.

On his way out of the church, Stanley stopped in the prayer room. It was quiet. Seemed soft, perhaps because of the carpeted floor and the cushioned chairs. He prayed at home every day, but there was something he really liked about praying in that little room—like he was closer to God's ear or something.

And it was usually empty. Same story tonight.

Stanley kneeled down in front of the lone pew. Set his elbows on the bench and folded his hands in front of his face. "Lord, You know my heart. You know I…I really didn't know how to be a father. Didn't have one, myself. But I'm not this bad, evil person. Well, maybe I used to be. But not anymore. And I thank You for changing me. Help me to be the person You see in me because I don't even really know what the new me even looks like. I know I'm supposed to look more like Jesus. I need to know Jesus more. Show me. Show me, Lord. In Jesus' name, Amen."

As he stood, the door to the prayer room opened.

"Oh, I'm sorry!"

Stanley recognized the pretty woman before him. Big brown eyes, short, curly hair, and a bubbly smile. She sang in the choir with an unmistakably beautiful hummingbird voice.

"No problem. I was just leaving." He nodded politely.

"You can stay," she offered with a grin. "I mean, God *is* every-where."

There was the smile. And she was looking into his eyes. Prob-ably trying to figure out if his eyes were really green or if he was wearing contact lenses.

Stanley turned on the charm with a smile of his own. "He sure is. And I'm sure He listens to a pretty woman like you. What's your name?"

Her eyebrow shot up as though he'd said something wrong. "Uh...my name is Debbie. But God listens to everybody, regard-less of how *man* views us."

Stanley's smile slipped to a straight lipped expression. *I'm a new man.* "My apologies. Didn't mean to offend."

"None taken."

And with that, Debbie left the prayer room.

Stanley laid his coat on the ground again and prayed a second prayer. "I'm back, God. These old habits die hard. I need You. Amen."

CHAPTER 3

Yolanda listened attentively as she waited for the Child Support hotline to reveal her balance. She'd already called twice this week and no deposit had been made. She'd assumed there was a delay because of the Christmas holiday.

The automated voice said, "Your balance is two dollars and forty-five cents. Your last deposit of three hundred forty-five dollars was made on November 1, 2016. Press the star key to hear more transactions or the pound key for more options."

Dang, still nothing. Out of frustration Yolanda threw her phone on the coffee table and sat on the living room couch. This wasn't the first time she'd been disappointed about not receiving her child support. Her kids' father, Jesse, was always in between jobs. It seemed like every time she reported his job change to the child support office, he'd switch employers again. Yolanda assumed he had grown tired of running and would stay on his most recent job, since she'd been getting money for six months now.

In her mind, she blamed the R&B group Jodeci. She'd met Jesse at one of their concerts. Jesse didn't waste any time putting his mack down on her. Yolanda giggled as she remembered the lame line he used to get her attention.

"Say, baby, you got them eyes that'll make me give up my whole check."

Yolanda had blushed because she'd never had a guy pay her any attention. Jesse was her first boyfriend, first love, first everything.

After dating for a few months, she got pregnant with Deontae. Jesse was upset because he wanted his son named after him.

But Gwen, Yolanda's mother, told her that a woman should never name a child Junior unless they were married. "He didn't give you his last name, so you ain't puttin' his first name on your baby."

Two years after Deontae, Yolanda got pregnant with Eric. Jesse tried to talk her into having an abortion. He said he didn't want any more kids, but the truth of the matter was that he had another baby on the way. Yolanda was upset for a while, but then got back with him after he promised never to betray her again.

Two years after giving birth to Eric, Yolanda found herself pregnant again. This time with a girl, Zoey. Jesse didn't come to the hospital nor did he sign Zoey's birth certificate. He told Yolanda that he only made boys, so Zoey couldn't be his. Yolanda didn't argue with him. She filed for child support and told the judge she wanted a DNA test for all of her kids. The tests came back 99.9 percent Jesse Davis was indeed the father of all three. Right after she got those results, Jesse disappeared from their lives.

"You didn't have to bring the white man into our business!" he had fumed during their last conversation. "I feel like a slave to the system now!"

She'd reminded him that this wouldn't have happened if he'd kept his word and continued to support his children in the first place.

But Jesse wasn't hearing it. He had stomped away from her doorstep without looking back.

Classic, typical, sorry man. She sighed. There was nothing she could do about Jesse now except continue to chase him down like a bill-collector.

She stood up from the couch. "Ouch!" Yolanda plucked a Lego from her foot. She threw the hard plastic to the floor.

"Deontae, Eric, and Zoey, get y'all butts in here and clean up this living room!"

The children rushed to her call. "Mama, Eric called me fat," Zoey whined.

"No I didn't. I said you was *big*."

"That's the same thing, you stupid," Deontae added.

"All of y'all hush and clean up. I don't wanna hear any arguing. I'm not in the mood today."

Yolanda and her kids shared a small, three-bedroom home with her mother, Gwen. Although the house was in the "good" part of town, it wasn't Yolanda's dream house. The living room was almost smaller than a doctor's waiting room. Gwen was a hoarder so the walls were cluttered. She had a picture of every President on the wall, a Martin Luther King church fan, a picture of Jesus and His disciples at the last supper, and a calendar from Morgan and Jackson Funeral Home. The living room also had a 32-inch TV with a stand, a coffee table with wobbling legs, a dingy brown couch, and was surrounded by several plants.

Yolanda wanted her own space, but with her temporary job at Metro DXM she couldn't afford to move out. She'd been working there three months and just finished training. Her goal was to become permanent, make supervisor, and then get her own place.

"Mama, can we go get some ice cream when we finish?" Zoey asked, picking up the last of the toys.

"Naw, we can't get no ice cream. We can't get *nothing*. I don't have no money for nothing extra. I can barely pay for what you *need* as it is, let alone a *want* like ice cream. Maybe if I had some help around here…" Yolanda fought back the tears that were forming in her eyes.

Deontae winced but continued wiping furniture polish onto the coffee table.

"See, now you done made Mama mad," Eric pointed out.

"I'm sorry, Mommy." Zoey pouted.

"Baby, I'm not mad at you. It's not your fault. Give me a hug." Yolanda pulled Zoey into her arms and held her tight. This time, Yolanda couldn't stop the tears from flowing like a river. She cried for her children and she cried for herself. Her kids were her world and she was doing the best that she could for them. Sometimes, however, it just didn't seem like enough.

From time to time Deontae would ask about their dad. Yolanda couldn't tell them the real truth. She'd told him that Jesse worked overseas. Deontae questioned why he never flew home or called to check on them. Yolanda told him that flying was expensive and so was calling home when a person was in another country.

"Mama, why are you crying?" Eric asked.

"I'm okay, Eric. Just having a bad day. Take your sister to my bedroom and y'all can watch a movie."

"Can we watch SpongeBob instead?" Zoey asked.

"Man, that's for babies." Eric frowned.

"Eric, just put the TV on Cartoon Network since that's the channel you and Zoey watch all the time," Deontae suggested.

"That'll work," Eric said and Zoey agreed.

At age thirteen, Deontae was a great help with his siblings. He could check homework and even whip up a few simple meals in the kitchen.

"Thanks, D."

"You're welcome, Mama. Are you alright?"

"I'm going to be fine, baby. Run this trash to the curb for me."

Deontae took the trash bag and went outside.

With the children out of view, Yolanda's brain returned to the crisis of the day. She only had a few hours left before Gwen got off work and a few hours before time to pay the electric bill. Yolanda had the bulk of the money, but she was still $65 short. She had been depending on her child support check to bring up the rear.

She could hear Gwen fussing now: *Don't count money that ain't in your hand.*

Think. Think. What can I do for money? She had already sold every extra book in the house to a resale bookstore. She already had two payday loans out. She'd promised the kids that she wouldn't take any more of their electronics to the pawn shop.

Times like these, Yolanda almost wished she had a sugar daddy. Shoot, she'd take a *flour* daddy right now. If she had any kind of daddy at all, maybe she wouldn't be in this predicament.

The only connection she had to her father was her paternal grandmother, and today, she'd have to do.

Retrieving her cell phone from the coffee table, Yolanda called Grandma Effie. On the third ring, Grandma Effie answered, "Hello."

"Hey, Grandma. It's Yolanda. How are you?"

"Oh baby, I'm fine. How you and them babies doing?"

"Ummm…we…we're okay." Yolanda stuttered. She had only asked her grandma for money once, to get a prescription for Zoey's asthma medicine. Yolanda had hurriedly paid Grandma Effie back and never asked to borrow money again.

"You don't sound fine. What's the matter, baby?"

"My electricity will be disconnected if I don't pay the bill today before five. I'm sixty-five dollars short. Can I borrow the money and pay you back next Friday when I get my check?" Yolanda took a deep breath and waited on Grandma Effie to reply.

"Chile, of course you can borrow the money. I can't let you and them babies be in the dark."

"Thanks, Grandma Effie. I promise I'll pay you back."

"I know you will, baby."

"Okay, I'll come by and pick up the money after while."

Yolanda and Grandma Effie said their goodbyes and Yolanda finally exhaled easily. They would make it through another week.

Yolanda knew not to mention going to Grandma Effie's house to Gwen. Gwen was still bitter behind her breakup with Yolanda's father, Stanley. Gwen and Stanley met in college and once she got pregnant with Yolanda, things changed. Stanley left college and Gwen. According to Gwen, Stanley said he wasn't ready to be a father.

Yolanda vaguely remembered him. She'd only seen Stanley once or twice. Due to his lack of participation in Yolanda's life, Gwen had raised Yolanda by herself. Gwen had made sure Yolanda knew exactly how trifling her father and his family were. "His momma sitting up there in that two-story house. That woman could have sent me something on behalf of her ig-nut son! And his sister got a college degree, I know she could afford to send something!"

Despite Gwen's attempts to paint all the Brown family in a bad light, Grandma Effie made it her business to keep up with Yolanda, especially since Yolanda was her first grandchild. Grandma Effie sent Yolanda money on her birthday. Gwen would make snide remarks under her breath, "Must be nice to give a gift once a year like Santa Claus."

Still, Yolanda appreciated what Grandma Effie did. She and her kids would drop by to see Grandma Effie every once in a while because Yolanda had no hard feelings against her grandmother.

Her father, however, was a different story.

"Mama, can I go down the street and play football with Reggie and Zack?" Deontae asked as he entered the living room.

"You can when we get back. Go get your sister and brother. We gotta make a quick run."

Yolanda packed her kids in the car and headed to Big Oak, a 45-minute drive from Jaxton. She barely had enough gas to make it there and back, but she had to make this work. Time was also of the essence. Her plan was to get the money, stop by and pay the electricity bill, and head back to fix dinner before Gwen made it home.

Yolanda pulled in front of Grandma Effie's brick home. She couldn't help but notice the well-manicured yard. She assumed Grandma Effie must have paid someone for the upkeep of the yard. The hedges were perfectly trimmed, grass cut nicely, and a beautiful flowerbed full of blooming perennials.

"Deontae, go to the door and tell Grandma Effie you're picking up my package. Tell her we're pushed for time, but we'll stay longer next time."

"I wanna see Grandma Effie," Zoey whined.

"Yeah me, too," Eric chimed in.

"Okay, all of y'all can go, but hurry up."

"Okay," they all said in unison and hopped out of the car.

The children loved visiting their Grandma Effie because she always had a treat for them. If it wasn't some of her baked goodies, she'd give them a few dollars to buy a treat.

Yolanda turned the Honda Accord's ignition off to conserve gas. She kept the radio going as she listened to Z98.4. *Dance With My Father* by Luther Vandross came on. *Umph at least they had a chance to do one dance with their father, I can't even get a phone call.* She sighed. Every time she thought of Stanley, she had to fight to keep from being overcome by sadness. What upset her even more was the thought that her children would spend their lives fighting it, too.

She turned off the radio. *Stupid song.*

Suddenly, Eric came running out the house smiling and waving his arms like he'd hit the lottery. "Mama, Paw-paw here! He say get out."

"You don't have a paw-paw, Eric. Are you talking about one of your Grandma Effie's friends from church?"

"No, ma'am. It's *our* Paw-paw." He smiled. "Your Daddy!"

Yolanda's body froze. Her eyes scanned to the street. There was a car parked in the driveway she didn't recognize. Aunt Emily had moved. Maybe her father *was* there.

"Go get Deontae and Zoey and tell them to come on," Yolanda ordered in a panic. She cranked up the car's ignition.

"But Mama—"

"Do what I told you to do. Now!" she yelled, cutting him off.

Yolanda's heart was beating so fast and hard it felt like it was going to jump out of her chest. Was it really her father? Why didn't Grandma Effie tell her?

She could feel heat rising inside of her and small beads of sweet forming on her forehead.

Just as she was about to blow the horn the younger kids came out with a tall, dark man in tow. All it took was the light hitting his green eyes a certain way to verify that this man was, indeed, her father.

"Mom, here's the package from Grandma Effie," Deontae said as he handed her a sealed envelope and got in the car. He rolled his passenger's side window down so that Stanley could talk to Yolanda.

Eric and Zoey got in the backseat.

"Hurry up and put your seatbelts on so I can drive off," Yolanda nearly screamed. But they weren't moving fast enough.

Stanley stuck his head inside the window. "Yolanda, how's it going?"

Yolanda couldn't look into his eyes directly. She focused, instead, on his lips. They were slightly upturned, like a goofy grin. She wished she could reach across Deontae and smack her father for asking such a casual question.

She spoke to his mouth. "How's it going? How dare you walk out to my car and ask me how's it going like we see each other all the time. You're really a piece of work, and you even have the audacity to tell my kids to call you Paw-paw. Wow. Unfreaking believable! My mother was right about you. All you care about is yourself."

His grin had slipped away. "Yolanda, I'm a changed man."

She turned her gaze to the steering wheel. "Yeah right. The only thing you've probably changed is your clothes."

"I know you're upset, but please hear me out," Stanley begged.

"I've heard enough. Now please get away from my car before I run you over," she spat.

Yolanda rolled up the window and sped off before Stanley could reply.

CHAPTER 4

Yolanda felt like she was in a twilight zone. Her head was spinning. She was high-tailing it back to Jaxton as though being chased by a madman.

At one point, she'd wanted to cry, but then she got angry all over again. Her stomach began to flutter and she felt like she needed to puke. She quickly pulled into the Big Ace's Convenience store parking lot.

"Deontae, go into the store and get me a bottle of water," she said, handing him the money.

Yolanda rolled down the window to get some fresh air. She couldn't catch her breath.

The churning in her stomach gave her warning of what was to come. She hurriedly opened the door and released the bile that was forcing its way out.

Eric jumped out of the car and ran to give her aid.

"Do I need to call the ambulance, Mama?"

"Just look in the glove compartment and get me some napkins."

Nine year old Zoey's eyes filled with tears. "Mama, are you going to die?"

"Zoey, sweetheart, I'm going to be just fine. I'm sure it's just something I ate," she replied, wiping her mouth.

"Dang, Mama, you sprayed the parking lot good," Deontae said as he got back in the car.

Eric barked, "Deontae, this ain't funny. Mama sick for real."

"She only threw up. You acting like she got hit by a car or

something." Eric bucked up to his older brother.

"Noooooo, I don't want Mama to get hit by a car," Zoey whimpered.

Yolanda interrupted their argument. "Alright that's enough. Y'all got Zoey all upset for nothing. D, gimme my water."

Deontae followed her orders while giving Eric the evil eye.

Yolanda gathered herself and took a swig of the bottle of water. She poured some of the water of her napkin and patted her face with it as well. When she finished, she took a good look at her children. The fear of seeing their mother sick was present in their six little eyes. This was no time to be having an emotional breakdown. She had to pull it together for her kids. She wasn't the first single mom to have to push her feeling aside in order to deal with life, and she wouldn't be the last. "Let's not talk about Paw-paw anymore."

After wiping all traces of anguish from her face, Yolanda told the children to wait in the car while she went inside and got the money order for the electricity bill. Inside the store, she kept her smile plastered in place. She filled out the money order and joined her kids in the car again.

Zoey and Eric were arguing over a bag of cookies.

"Where did you guys get cookies?" Yolanda fussed as she grabbed the Ziploc container.

"Grandma Effie gave 'em to us," Zoey said.

"She gave them to *me*," Deontae claimed.

"But they're for all of us," Eric explained.

"Well, they're not for anyone until after dinner," Yolanda said as she sat the bag inside her purse.

With the cookie argument settled, they rode on to the City of Jaxton Municipal Building. The kids waited on a wooden bench as Yolanda stood in line to pay the bill.

Then they headed back home. Yolanda started on dinner almost as soon as they walked in the door. Gwen would be home soon, and she made it known that whoever got home first in the evenings was obligated to start dinner.

Yolanda carried on with life as usual, as though the whole incident with her father had never happened.

But the kids remembered. "Mama, I thought you said Paw-paw was dead," Eric remarked. He was gathered at the kitchen table with his siblings doing homework while Yolanda cooked.

"He's not dead. We just saw him," Zoey stated.

"Both of you please be quiet. And whatever you do, don't mention any of this to your granny."

"Mama, I'm glad he ain't dead. It'll be cool to have him around to help me with my football skills," Deontae said.

Yolanda tapped her spoon on the edge of her pot. She pointed the spoon at her kids. "Listen. I don't want you guys getting your hopes up about your grandfather being in our lives. I don't know anything about him. I haven't seen him in years. So I don't want y'all getting all excited for nothing. Besides, he's probably just stopping by for a few days."

"Grandma Effie said he's living with her now," Deontae pointed out.

"Well, whatever. I told you already, I don't want to talk about him anymore. Do I make myself clear?" She raised her voice.

"Yes, ma'am," the children replied.

Yolanda honestly didn't know how she felt about seeing Stanley. For years she'd practiced what she would say if she ran into him. *Why didn't you care enough to be in my life? Where is my child support money? Why didn't you marry my mother?* None of those things came to mind when she saw him.

Even though she hadn't looked at him dead-on when he got to her car, she'd seen enough to know that she looked just like him. Grandma Effie had told her that she looked as if Stanley had spit her out and not Gwen. She thought it was an exaggeration on Grandma Effie's part but this wasn't the case. The two shared the same skin tone, same nose, and same eye color. That made Yolanda angry just thinking about it. She wanted no parts of Stanley Brown.

Yolanda's meal of spaghetti, corn on the cobb, salad, and crescent rolls was a favorite for the kids. Gwen didn't really care for spaghetti, but she'd eat it nonetheless. Yolanda was spent from the day, so she left the kids alone with Gwen when it was time to eat.

She had hoped that Gwen would be too tired for the kids' chit-chat, too, but when Gwen asked Zoey, "How's my favorite granddaughter doing?" Yolanda thought she'd better get up off the couch and pretend to clean up something so she could monitor the table conversation. Zoey was a bit of a motor mouth.

When there was a break in the table conversation, Yolanda asked, "Hey, Mom. How was work today?" She kept, rearranging the rack of *Ebony* magazines.

"Tough. This morning, I had a headache that I couldn't shake. Took almost until lunch before my Ibuprofen kicked in."

"Okay, well, that's terrible. You should go ahead and get in bed. You probably have too much on your mind."

Yolanda abandoned the magazines. She grabbed Gwen's empty plate and put it in the sink.

"I can clean up my own plate, thank you very much. Why you so jittery?"

"Mom, I'm not jittery, just trying to help you out, that's all."

"Granny, Mama sick, too. She was throwing up in the car," Zoey stated.

"Throwing up? What's going on with you?" Gwen crossed her arms and leaned back in her chair.

"It's nothing, Mom. I'm fine."

"Yolanda, I don't want no surprises, you hear me?" She frowned.

"I love surprises," Zoey added.

Yolanda paced the floor. "Mom, really, I'm fine."

"Granny, you want some of my cookies?" Zoey asked.

"No, baby. I don't want any cookies."

"Zoey, baby, why don't you go on outside with your brothers and play," Yolanda interjected.

"But I want to eat one of Grandma Effie's cookies for dessert," Zoey blurted out before exiting the room.

Everyone froze except Zoey, whose hand flew to cover her mouth. "Oops."

Gwen blinked her eyes slowly, then turned to Yolanda. "What's really going on?"

"Nothing, Mom. I told you—"

"Look, girl, I didn't just meet you yesterday. You're a horrible liar, so just spill it."

Yolanda rolled her eyes as she gathered her thoughts. "I went to go visit Grandma Effie and she gave the kids cookies."

"Yolanda, I want the whole truth and I want it now!" Gwen yelled.

"I went to Grandma Effie's house and my father was there," Yolanda answered.

"Let me get this straight. You went to see Effie and no-good Stanley was there, too? Why did you think you needed to keep that a secret from me?"

"I know how you feel about him, so I felt it best not to mention him."

"I don't know what his plan is, or what your plan is, but I don't want to be around him. I don't want to see him, and I certainly don't want him around my grandkids." Gwen pounded her fist on the counter top.

"You don't want who around us, Granny?" Eric asked as he entered the living room.

"Didn't I tell you to stay out of grown folks business?" Yolanda spat.

"Don't be yelling at Eric. He was talking to me. Eric, I don't want your no-good granddaddy around you. I don't want the sorry, I can't keep a job, can't pay a bill, spell to fall on you." Gwen rolled her neck as she spoke.

"Paw-paw was cool," Eric replied.

"Paw-paw? The world must be coming to an end. He ain't never even seen you and you calling the man Paw-paw. Lord have mercy, my head *really* hurting now. Elizabeth, I'm coming to join you." Gwen placed her hand over her heart, mimicking Fred Sanford.

"Mom, can we discuss this later?"

"There's nothing to discuss, I've said all I have to say. I'm very disappointed in you for telling my grandbaby to call him Paw-paw."

"I didn't tell him to call him Paw-paw. I wasn't in the house when they saw him. If I had known he was going to be there, I wouldn't have gone."

"What about what *we* want?" Eric asked.

"You're a child, you don't have sense enough to know what you want. Stay out of grown folks business," Gwen shouted. "I'm not going to let y'all run my pressure up."

Gwen stormed out of the living room and went to her bedroom and slammed the door.

CHAPTER 5

Stanley was still feeling rattled from Yolanda's reaction to seeing him two days ago. And this meeting tonight with the Deacon's Board had him messing up on the dock. He'd dropped several pallets in the wrong bins, loaded up a truck out of order, and felt a muscle pull in his lower back from lifting incorrectly. The thought of quitting the job entered his mind. *I'm too old for this. I'm overqualified for this job. They don't pay me enough to put up with this.*

But that would create a no-win situation. If he quit his job, he wouldn't have a source of money because, for now, he was womanless. Momma would let him stay in the house, but she wouldn't feed him. She was suddenly religious when it came to Stanley. "God said, if a man don't work, he shouldn't eat. And I can't go against the Bible."

Over the years, he'd been glad that the women who'd housed him had never read that alleged Scripture.

Is that in the Bible, anyway? Stanley wondered as he maneuvered the forklift into a parking position.

He clocked out at five on the dot. He had plans tonight. He had to get his mother, this job, and Yolanda out of his mind because the Deacon's Board had invited him to an interview.

Deacon Stanley Brown. The name had a nice cadence to it. Respectable. People would look at him differently.

Everybody except Yolanda. And Gwen. And the rest of his exes, but that was beside the point. If he were *Deacon* Brown, they'd have to at least acknowledge that he was doing the right thing now. He would get some business cards printed up and give them to his other daughters when he met them.

He made a bee-line home and sprinted into the shower. He put on his best gray suit with a crisp, white, textured shirt. His tie was mostly red, with rectangles of tan, blue, and white. He donned circular link cuffs, a Christmas gift from a woman whose name he couldn't even remember.

Despite his confident appearance, Stanley was a jumble of nerves. What would they ask? Why did they even need this interview? He had already been coming to church and putting money in the offering basket for two months straight now. What exactly did a Deacon do, anyway, besides sit on the side bench on Sunday mornings?

He decided to give his former pastor a call, hoping for a little more guidance.

"Hey, Brother Stanley. Good to hear from you." Pastor Willie Lee's voice bellowed before the first ring was even finished.

"Hello, Pastor. Sorry I've been out of touch. Been working a lot of overtime at my job." Stanley heard himself bragging.

"Yeah, that overtime is a killer. I bet the money is good, though, huh?"

"Yes, siree. I'm saving up a pretty penny."

"Good news indeed. What can I help you with?"

That was one thing Stanley liked about Pastor Lee. He was a man's man. Got straight to the point. No pretense, no dilly-dallying. "I'm being interviewed to become a Deacon at Warren Grove. Thought you might give me some tips to prepare."

"What you say, now! When's the interview?"

Stanley laughed. "In about thirty minutes."

"Alright, alright," Pastor Lee said with a slight laugh of his own. "They'll want to know about your experience with Christ."

"Got that." If Stanley knew nothing else, he could tell that testimony for the entire time.

"They'll want to know about your family. If you were raised in a Christian home, you know, Christian parents."

"Strike one," Stanley interrupted.

"It's not a strike if you weren't," Pastor Lee said. "They're just asking to see where they need to come in with training. Usually, people who grew up in the church are familiar with the by-laws and such already. But as a newer brother, they'll be sure to train you more thoroughly, that's all. I've been in fellowship with the men of Warren Grove a time or two. Don't worry."

Stanley sighed. "Okay. Jesus and my family background. What else?"

"They'll probably ask if you've been married. How many children you have, how they turned out."

"Strikes two and three. I can't..." Stanley stopped shy of telling Pastor Lee about what a failure he had been in relationships and as a father. The people at Lee Chapel hadn't cared so much about Stanley's past as what Christ was doing in him now. Pastor Lee, himself, had given his own testimony of how the Lord had changed him following his father's death. Shouldn't everyone just ask, "Where are you now?" not "What all did you do before you met Jesus?" That was the whole point of life in Jesus anyway, right?

But Stanley wasn't going to moan and complain about it. *It is what it is.*

"I'll do my best," he stated.

"Brother Stanley. Just tell the truth. And tell your testimony. All they can do is say yea or nay."

"True," Stanley agreed.

"And even if man says no, God has already said 'yes' to you, my brother. You don't have to be a Deacon to serve."

Stanley nodded. "Yeah. I hear you." *But Deacon Stanley Brown sure would look nice on that card.*

The meeting took place in the same fellowship hall where the brothers met one Saturday a month. But somehow, that same room took on a different aura when Stanley was sitting across from three men who were grilling him.

Brother Robertson wasn't there. Instead, the Pastor's assistant and two other Deacon's whom Stanley had only greeted in passing were present. They had forms, checklists, and a Bible sitting on the table when he walked in. Their tables weren't arranged in the usual friendly rows. They were in an L-shape, with Stanley seated on the short end.

"Good evening." Stanley shook their hands as they introduced themselves. Deacon Reed, Brother Berman, and Deacon Lewis, the head of the Deacon's Board.

He ain't even a Deacon. Why is he here?

"I'll open us up in prayer," Deacon Reed said matter-of-factly.

Stanley bowed his head as Deacon Reed, an elderly man dressed in a fashionable denim suit, prayed for guidance in the selection process. Then his tone got deeper. "And Lord God, we know that You know when people are *lying*. When they're trying to *cover up*. We pray that the truth and the truth only be spoken tonight. Let anyone who is lying tonight in this, your holy church, be smote down straight from Your throne. In Jesus' name. Amen."

"Amen?" Stanley heard himself questioning already.

"If it's all the same to you, we'll jump right in it," Deacon Reed said.

Stanley looked at Deacon Lewis and Brother Berman, hoping their faces would hint that this was some kind of pre-initiation joke because it certainly felt like one.

Their faces showed serious expressions.

"Sure. Fire away," Stanley agreed.

Deacon Lewis began, "When you die, are you going to heaven or hell, and why?"

"I'm going to heaven because Christ died for my sin and I've believed on Him for forgiveness." That was easy.

Deacon Lewis and Brother Berman both checked boxes on their forms.

Deacon Reed asked, "What about the Holy Ghost? You got the Holy Ghost with the evidence of speaking in tongues? Did you fast with the congregation at the beginning of the year?"

Before Stanley could try to answer, Deacon Lewis pointed toward the paper in front of Deacon Reed. "Let's stick to the questions, Deacon Reed."

The next questions applied to the ministry itself. How often would he be available to serve? Did he have a criminal record that might affect his ability to be insured? Did he have any community service experience?

Thankfully, Stanley breezed through those with his work schedule and availability, a firm no about the criminal history, and a sheer willingness to learn how to serve his community effectively.

Lewis and Berman's faces loosed up and the line of questioning felt more like a conversation than an interview now.

Charm pays off in various ways.

Stanley got the feeling that Reed was just a disagreeable person no matter what. Two out of three people voting for Stanley should be enough.

"Now. Your family," Reed jumped in.

Why did they leave those questions for him?

Stanley set his elbows on the table and laced his fingers.

Reed squinted, looking at Stanley's hands. "Not married, I see."

"No, sir."

Reed checked his paper hard. "Ever *been* married?"

"No, sir."

"Kids?"

"Yes. Three." Though Stanley realized the correct answer was four, he wanted to divulge as little information as possible.

Reed pushed his glasses up on his face. "Hmph." He wrote

something on his page. "Ages of children?"

Stanley's mind frantically searched to do the math. Todderick and Sabrina were the same age. They were, according to his mother, "ghetto twins" because they had been born within months of each other. "Twenty-two…" He stalled.

He wished his hands weren't on the table because he needed those fingers to count the years that must have been between Sabrina and Kim. *Hmmm…* He distinctly remembered signing the papers to relinquish parental rights the day after the Cowboys won their last Super Bowl, which was in 1995. He remembered feeling elated about the win, yet crushed that Kim's mother, Sherry, had gotten married and moved on. That was the first time a woman had closed the door permanently on him. Let's see, *1995 was twenty-two years ago. She was eight at the time.* "My middle daughter is thirty."

Deacon Reed's eyebrows were closing in.

Stanley prayed that God wasn't in a smoting mood because he was going to have to make his best guess about Yolanda's age. "My oldest is thirty-four?"

"Are you asking me or telling me?" Deacon Reed commanded.

"I'm saying she's thirty-four." Stanley tried to sound more sure of himself this time, but his face must have gave the uncertainty away.

"Brother Brown," Deacon Lewis said as he leaned forward, "do you have relationships with your immediate family members?"

"Oh, yes," Stanley piped up. "I moved back home to take care of my mother. She's stable, but she needs someone with her. And my sister, Emily, why…I just had a good talk with her the other day. I have uncles, cousins, you know. I saw them on the holidays, if I happened to come home."

"What about your children?" Brother Berman wanted to know.

He shook his head. "No. I don't know them well. Relationships with their mothers went bad. Lost touch. So I don't know them very well."

"You don't know them *well* or at all?" Deacon Reed pressed.

Stanley took a deep breath. That man was determined to get the dirt. "At all."

"I see," Deacon Lewis said.

Deacon Reed made no attempt to hide the big "X" he wrote across the paper he'd been using to take notes. He dropped his pen on the table, crossed his arms, and leaned back in his chair.

"We do appreciate your honesty," Brother Berman said. "We've all made mistakes in the past. Can't think of a man alive who hasn't messed up at least one relationship."

Deacon Lewis nodded slightly. "Amen."

Not a word from Deacon Reed.

"We will take your interest into consideration. Thank you for taking the time to meet with us today." Deacon Lewis stood.

Stanley and the rest stood as well. He extended his hand to each of them. Since these were men that he'd have to see Sunday after Sunday, Stanley decided he might as well make a joke of this meeting. "Let me guess. Don't call us, we'll call you, right?"

Deacon Reed busted out laughing. He slapped Stanley on the shoulder. "You got a good sense of humor, I'll give you that."

Lewis and Berman laughed only slightly. "We take every interest into prayerful consideration, Brother Brown. God has the final say."

"Thank you," Stanley said as he let himself out the church's back door.

Once outside, he let the cool winter air seep deep into his lungs. *Whew! That was a nightmare. Worse than a trip to the principal's office.* But he was glad he'd done it. It felt good to confess, even though it probably cost him a position at the church.

He needed a juicy burger after all that.

Booker's Burgers still stood on the corner of King and Caldwell streets. Mr. Booker had passed away, but his son and daughter kept the place going. There had been a few close calls with the IRS

35

and the health department, but the neighborhood always rallied to keep the store open when needed.

Stanley found a parking spot behind the tiny restaurant. The welcomed smell of frying grease met him at the door. The cashier, a young man who had to be related to the Booker family by the look of his wide nose and pointy forehead, asked, "How can I help you?"

Quickly, Stanley scanned the hand-written menu on the overhead chalkboard. "Let me get a number one with cheese."

"Fries and a drink?"

"Yeah. I'm goin' all in tonight."

The young man smiled, showing his full gold grill. He pressed a few buttons on the ancient cash register. "That'll be seven dollars and fourteen cents."

"Man," Stanley said as he fished his wallet from his back pocket. "I remember when I used to pay three dollars for this exact same meal."

"Been a long time, sir."

"What—you trying to say I'm old?" Stanley teased.

"I mean…if the whole meal was three dollars…I'm just sayin'."

"Young man, you just messed up your tip."

"Aww man!"

Stanley smiled. "I'm just messin' with you." He put two dollars in the glass tip jar.

"Thank you, sir." He handed Stanley the bottom portion of an ordering slip and a cup for the drink. "Number forty-seven."

Stanley made his drink and took a seat near the pick-up counter. As he sipped the cold soda, he read through the tabletop dessert menu. Strawberry cake. Peach cobbler. Sweet potato pies. He couldn't make himself a regular here like he'd done back in the day when his metabolism burned up everything he consumed. Good thing that was probably his first and last Deacon's Board meeting.

He heard a woman's voice say, "How you doin', prayin' man?"

He looked up to see the hummingbird lady, Debbie, standing over him.

"Pretty good. You?"

"Same." She stepped to the large, steel container marked "Sweet Tea" and filled her Styrofoam cup. She held an order slip in her hand, too.

"Have a seat?" Stanley asked, motioning toward the empty chair across from him.

"If you don't mind."

"No problem," he said.

"You eat here often?"

"No. Only when I've got problems."

"Problems?" She took the bait.

Stanley took another sip of his drink. "The church is looking to add some more deacons. I had an interview tonight."

Her face lit up, just like he'd wanted people's faces to light up with the news that he was a respected man. "That's great. How is it a problem?"

"Man, they asked me more questions than I had to answer when I got my job."

She smiled. "I suppose they need to."

Stanley rubbed his inner elbow. "And my arm still hurts from where they took the blood sample."

Debbie's face scrunched in. Her eyes squinted. "They did *not* take your blood."

He chuckled. "No, but they might as well have."

"Number forty-eight," a girl yelled from the pick-up area.

"Wait…how's your food ready before mine?" Stanley asked as Debbie stood.

"I just got a salad." She grabbed her purse straps from the back of her chair. "Nice seeing you."

"Nice date," Stanley suggested.

"I wouldn't exactly call that a date." Debbie snarked.

"We'll have to do something about that."

"Forty-eight."

"Bye, prayin' man." Debbie dismissed herself. "I'm sure every-thing will work out for the best. It always does for those who love Him."

That sounded like a Scripture, which totally threw Stanley off his game.

"Good night," was all he managed to say.

CHAPTER 6

Three days had passed since Yolanda saw Stanley. A part of her halfway wished that he would contact her to prove that he honestly wanted to be in her life.

Who am I fooling? He's just like Jesse. She sighed.

She checked her Facebook page to see if her sister, Kim, had said anything about Stanley.

Yolanda met her sister, Kim Maxwell, in an online jazz group. The two became friends and because of their unbelievable resemblance they both suspected that they were related. Grandma Effie not only confirmed that they were related, she told them they were sisters.

Kim wasn't the same complexion as Yolanda but she had those strong Brown family genes. She also had the light green eyes.

Unlike Yolanda, Kim grew up with a father. Not *their* father, but at least she had *a* father. Stanley gave up his rights so that Kim's stepfather, Louis Maxwell, could adopt her.

Yolanda looked through Kim's pictures and every photo showed her with her parents. Happy. Family picnics, vacations, church outings, dinners, etc. Every photo was full of love.

Yolanda didn't see anything about Stanley on Kim's page so she decided to call her.

"Hey, Yolanda. How's it going?" Kim asked.

"Girl, I'm okay. Same stuff different day."

"How are the kids?"

"They good."

"Cool, so what's going on?"

"I saw our father at Grandma Effie's house the other day. Did you know he was living with her now?"

Kim quizzed, "No, I had no idea. What did you say to him?"

"I didn't say anything to him. I just drove off."

"Why didn't you say something?" Kim asked.

"I was caught off guard."

"Yolanda, that was your opportunity to say everything that you've been wanting to say to him."

"So how do you feel now that you know he's here?"

"I honestly don't feel anything. I don't really know him," Kim said flatly.

"I don't know him either, but that doesn't stop me from being mad about him abandoning me." Yolanda feelings began to stir.

"I understand that you're upset. Maybe you can arrange to meet with him so you guys can talk," Kim suggested. "What did he look like? Is he married? Do we look like him?" Kim asked.

"For a person that don't really care, you sure have a lot of questions." Yolanda laughed.

"Well, I've always wondered if I look more like him since I don't look like my mom at all."

"You look like him, and I'm his twin."

"Wow, that's pretty cool! You're his twin," she said, trying to stay positive.

"Kim, how is that *cool*? I look like a man that don't care nothing about me," Yolanda fussed.

"In fairness to him, I think you should hear him out. You only know your mother's side of the story."

"Well her side is true. He left, didn't contact me, don't know nothing about me."

"Just think about it."

"I've already made up my mind. I'll talk with you later."

"Okay and I'll be praying that you change your mind."

"That's a prayer that won't get answered," Yolanda said and hung up the phone before Kim could respond.

CHAPTER 7

"Joyful, joyful, Loooord! We adore thee…" Debbie's melodious voice floated around the sanctuary via the Warren Grove's sound system. The speakers and sound weren't stellar, but Debbie's sweet notes were nonetheless heartfelt. In Stanley's opinion, Debbie didn't need a microphone. She didn't need a choir or an instrument, either. He would have been just fine listening to her sing a cappella.

He recognized that song from one of his mother's favorite movies, "Sister Act II". Momma watched that movie at least once a week—on a VHS player. Even though he was tired of hearing the entire plot play from his Momma's bedroom, he always stopped what he was doing and listened on two parts—when Lauryn Hill and that other girl sang at the piano, and Lauryn's solo at the beginning of their performance in the big contest. And just like he wished those kids hadn't come on stage when Lauryn Hill was singing the final song, he almost despised the choir now for interrupting Debbie's part. Especially that woman on the front row who could not catch a note, let alone hold it. Stanley was no singer, but he knew bad singing when he heard it.

If Stanley ever got close enough to Debbie, and if she should ever ask what he thought of the choir, he would tell her right away to put that woman on the back row.

Debbie's face always appeared somber when she sang. Resolute. But when she locked eyes with his that morning, Stanley could have sworn he saw a smile. A twinkle. It was just enough to give him the green light.

He took notes during the sermon so that he could review them later in the week every day before going to work. He had gotten into the habit of recording the Scriptures and main points, organizing them into five segments so that he would have something to re-read and think about for five days a week. The way things were going at his job with all the overtime, he might have to think of six. Maybe he could take the words of that song and meditate on them if he ended up working Saturday again. *Yeah, that's it. I'll think of Debbie singing that song.*

Stanley didn't scuttle out of the building as soon as they were dismissed. He hung around a bit longer, fiddling with his Bible and nodding good-bye to people, chit-chatting casually. All the while keeping an eye on Debbie, who was slowly making her way from the choir stand to the main doors. She, too, was talking to fellow congregants. Their conversations seemed more genuine, though.

Maybe one of these days Stanley would know these people, too. Especially after he became a deacon. *Oh-wait. That's over. Never mind.* He wouldn't be able to impress Debbie with his commitment to church. And he wasn't operating in his usual Mack-Daddy M.O. He would just have to be...himself. Whoever that was. *I'm in Christ now*, he reminded himself. That might be all the hope he had with Debbie, but having that common ground with Jesus just might do the trick.

Bible at his side, Stanley arranged to casually stride up alongside Debbie as she exited through the swinging wooden doors. "We meet again," he said as though he hadn't planned it all along.

"I see," Debbie said. Her smile wasn't quite as big as he'd hoped for.

He held the door open for her. "Ladies first."

"Thank you."

Debbie breezed past him. And kept walking. She nodded at a few more people, pulling her car keys out of her purse.

Stumped, Stanley all but chased her to the parking lot. "Um...

hey…I was wondering if you'd like to catch lunch together."

Debbie didn't look at him. She pressed a button on her key fob. "I-I'll have to pass, Brother Brown."

Stanley noted the blinking lights and clicking sound coming from a late model Corolla. Just the kind of car he'd expect from a sensible woman like Debbie. But her actions were nothing like what he'd expected.

"Wait." Stanley put a hand against her door before she could open it. "Did I…do something wrong?" *Doesn't she see all this Jesus in me?*

Debbie finally stopped long enough to look at him. Her brown eyes seemed heavy. She opened her mouth to say something, then stopped short of uttering the words that were obviously on her mind.

"What is it?" he asked. "I'm a man. I can take it. Plus, see, I got this Bible, so I can't say or do anything crazy." He held the Word up to his chest.

She grinned slightly. "Stanley, I'm not one to gossip. But I did overhear some choir members talking. And I heard something that, in all honesty, disturbs me."

Stanley's head shifted a little to the right. "Okaaaay?" He hardly knew anyone at the church. And pretty much everyone who had grown up in Warren Grove back in his day had had the good sense to leave for greener pastures. None of his exes lived in the town. The world wasn't *that* small, was it?

Debbie bit her lip.

Stanley tapped his chest with the Bible. "I'm safe."

She exhaled. "All right. I'm just going to say it. I think it's really sad that you don't have relationships with your three children. The time and effort it takes to pursue me would be better spent pursuing your own flesh and blood. Okay?"

"But…I can explain," Stanley tried.

"Explain yourself to your children," she said. "And please step away from my car."

He obeyed.

"Thank you," Debbie said as she proceeded to enter her car and drive away.

Stanley stood flat-footed and dumbfounded. *How did she... Deacon Reed.* He answered his own question before he had a chance to finish it.

He marched back into the church and found several people presumably straightening up the sanctuary after service. Among them, of course, were the deacons, ushers, and people he recognized as the hospitality committee from a few of the after-church fundraising dinners.

Deacon Reed was folding up chairs in the choir stand.

Stanley clutched the Bible in his hand extra hard. Were it not for the Word that had already taken root in him, Stanley might have said something to Deacon Reed. Yet, he couldn't just accuse the man without proof. Stanley hadn't memorized any Scriptures about how to organize a church because he would ask to be called home to glory before taking on the role of a pastor. But he had read enough of the New Testament to know there was a proper chain of commands in a church. Add to that his experience working at his job for the past few months and actually staying employed through a few run-ins with fellow employees. Stanley knew that he needed to speak to the head Deacon first.

"Deacon Reed." Stanley approached the man.

"Brother Brown. Good to see you." Deacon Reed stood tall. His shiny red suit was ridiculously loud. If there were a fashion standard for being a deacon, surely he never would have been allowed on the board.

"Is Deacon Lewis still here?"

"Yeah. He's ahead of me, taking these chairs back to the fellowship hall."

"Thank you."

Stanley hurried on to the church's kitchen and found the head Deacon doing exactly what Deacon Reed stated. "Can I help you?" he asked.

"Sure thing, man. Thanks."

"Yeah," Stanley said. He laid the Bible on a table, took a few chairs from Deacon Lewis's hand, and spread them open in the row that had already been started. "I need to talk to you for a second."

"Go right ahead."

Stanley straightened up the last few chairs. He waited until he had Deacon Lewis's attention.

"What's on your mind, Brother Brown?"

The two stood face-to-face.

"That interview took a lot out of me," Stanley began, "but I didn't think it would take my *dignity* away."

"Excuse me?"

"Someone who was in our private meeting went back and told other people about the status of my relationship with my children." Stanley tried hard to keep his tone steady, but in truth he wished he could yell and punch somebody.

"Whoa, hold your horses. How do you know somebody repeated something said in our meeting?"

"Because they knew exactly how many children I had. Before now, anyone who really knew my business would have said that I had *four* kids. But now, I only have..." Stanley fought hard to control his emotions. *Todderick is dead.* "Now, I only have *three* left. And the person who repeated this information to me knew exactly how many kids I have."

Deacon Lewis nodded. "First off, my condolences on your loss."

"Thank you."

"And let me apologize on behalf of the church for the breach of trust that might have taken place. I—"

"You know, it's things like this—people talking about people, spreading rumors, and dragging people's names through the dirt— that cause people to not set foot in a church. It took a lot for me to even walk into a house of God after all I did in the past. Seems like people out there on the streets and in the club will forgive me quicker than church folk will," Stanley fumed. "You don't know how hard it is to come to church when you've failed your own flesh and blood."

Deacon Lewis shook his head. "Don't flatter yourself, Brother Brown. We've *all* fallen short. Don't let the devil convince you that what you've done is any worse than what any one of us did in the eyes of the Lord."

Stanley shut his mouth because what he said almost sounded exactly like what Pastor Lee would have said.

"Like I said, I'm sorry about the information leak. I *will* get to the bottom of it. But in the meantime, *you* need to be restored from the guilt and shame of your past so that if someone does ever try to throw it in your face again, you can tell them—from your heart—what a Savior we have in Christ."

Stanley laughed under his breath. "If they give you a chance."

Deacon Lewis clapped Stanley on the back. "They will, my brother. God will make a way for you to share your testimony. Maybe you can share it with your children first."

Relaxed by Deacon Lewis's words and friendly gesture, Stanley's shoulders loosened. "I gotta tell you, Deacon Lewis, I'm old school. You know—my kids are grown. I was taught that when you turn eighteen, you strike out on your own, especially if you're a boy. Turn the page. Move out of your momma's house and get your own life. Your folks are done raising you. I don't even know how to begin with my children now that they are adults. It's like I missed out. No turning back, you know?"

"And where did you get that philosophy?" Deacon Lewis asked.

"It's just...how I was raised," Stanley replied.

46

"But you're helping your mother now, right?"

"Yes. And my sister helped before she and her husband had to move to Detroit."

"Then maybe families were meant for a lifetime. Not just eighteen years," Deacon Lewis suggested. "Just pray about it. God will show you."

Metal chairs clanked as Deacon Reed struggled to enter the room.

Without thinking, Stanley joined Deacon Lewis as they rushed to help the older man with his load.

"I should have known you two would be in here lolly-gagging."

"No. Brother Brown and I were just having a little talk."

"I repeat, lolly-gagging."

That ain't all you repeat, Stanley thought.

Deacon Lewis turned to Stanley. "I'll get an answer. Today. And I'll handle it."

"An answer to what?" Deacon Reed wanted to know.

"Glad you asked. Me, you, and Brother Berman need an emergency meeting. Right now," Deacon Lewis ordered.

Stanley dismissed himself from the room without another word.

CHAPTER 8

Yolanda couldn't wait for five o'clock to come so she could clock out and go home. The last five minutes of the day seemed to be taking their sweet time. It was the weekend and all she wanted to do was go home and relax.

Her days were long and her nights sleepless. She'd been dreaming about Stanley. Last night she'd dreamed they were at a carnival riding every ride there. He'd spent lots of money trying to win her a teddy bear. After several attempts, he finally gave up and just paid the guy for the teddy bear. Yolanda was giddy with excitement. She acted as if she had just won a trip to Disney. She reached to get the bear from him and he backed away. The closer she got, the further away he became, and before she knew it, he had disappeared.

What's wrong with me? Why am I still thinking about him? The tapping on her desk brought her back to reality.

"Yolanda, dang girl. You can't hear?" her co-worker, Tammi, asked.

Sidney, added, "Yeah, she over here day dreaming. Girl, who you thinking about?"

Yolanda fake-laughed at their questions. "What do y'all want?"

"Sidney and I are going to Lixxi's for happy hour. You wanna roll?"

"Thanks for the invite, but I have other plans."

"I knew you were over here thinking about your man. Tell us all about it." Sidney high- fived Tammi.

"I don>t have a new man. If I did, I wouldn't tell you two."

Sidney was known as the office gossip; she stayed in everybody's business. "Girl, you can tell me. I won't tell nobody."

Yolanda rolled her eyes.

"Well, man or not, I think you should come. It'll be fun," Tammi pointed out.

"Maybe next time. I really can't go tonight. I already have plans."

"Alright, suit yourself. See you on Monday," Tammi said.

"Have fun with your new boo," Sidney teased.

Tammi and Sidney left to clock out. Yolanda logged off her computer and headed to clock out as well.

The truth of the matter is that she would have loved to go to happy hour, but she didn't have anyone to help her out with her kids. Having girlfriends was something she didn't have time for. Gwen had made it clear that she was not a baby sitter or a taxi driver. So Yolanda didn't have anyone to pick Deontae up from basketball practice or anyone to pick Zoey up from aftercare day-care. Eric caught the bus home with their neighbor, Kendrick, and stayed with Kendrick and his mom until Yolanda got home from work.

It was bad enough that Yolanda had begged Gwen to pick Zoey up today. "I have a mandatory meeting after work," she had lied to Gwen. Yolanda couldn't tell Gwen that she was going to pay the money back to Grandma Effie.

The traffic flow from Jaxton to Big Oak wasn't as bad as Yolanda had expected it to be. When she arrived at Grandma Effie's house and saw that there was no car in the driveway, Yolanda breathed a sigh of relief.

She got out the car and practically ran to the door. She didn't want to take any chances on seeing Stanley. She definitely didn't want him to pull up and block her in. Then she'd be trapped and forced to deal with him.

"Baby, Effie ain't home," Ms. Bernice, the next-door neighbor, yelled from her porch.

"Do you know when she'll be back?"

"I don't know, baby. She must be low sick 'cause the a-ma-lance came and got her."

"Oh, no. Do you know what happened to her?"

"I don't really know, just saw them take her on that stretcher when I was out here getting my mail. It must've been the Lord telling me to come get it earlier 'cause I normally wait 'til my stories go off. I normally watch All My Children—"

"Ms. Bernice, I don't mean to cut you off. Can you please tell me what street the hospital is on?"

"The hospital is over on Shearton. It's right down the street from the Windmill Diner. I worked there several years. I was the head cook. Course that was a long time ago. I loved working there. People lined up for my oxtails." She smiled as though there was no emergency at hand.

"Thank you, Ms. Bernice," Yolanda said and hopped in the car. It was clear to her that Ms. Bernice was going to be just like the energizer bunny, keep going and going and going as long as possible.

Yolanda decided to text Kim to see if she could meet her there. Kim lived on the outskirts of Big Oak in Carlosville, which was less than a twenty-minute drive.

Kim texted her back stating that she was substituting at Big Oak High School and could meet her there.

With Big Oak being a small town, finding the hospital wouldn't be hard. The GPS on Yolanda's phone told her she would arrive in eight minutes. She followed the turn-by-turn directions. She and Kim arrived at the same time.

"Hey, sis. What happened to Grandma Effie?" Kim asked frantically.

"I'm really not sure. Ms. Bernice didn't say."

Yolanda and Kim rushed through the emergency room door and found the information desk. Big Oak Memorial reeked of

Lysol and bleach. The walls paint was peeling but there were beautiful framed pieces of art on the walls. Each painting had an *In Memory of* plate engraved on it.

"We're looking for Effie Mae Brown," Kim told the clerk who appeared to be watching a TV show on her cell phone.

"Ummm one moment please," they woman said as she popped some fruity smelling gum.

Yolanda side-eyed Kim as they waited.

"She's around the corner behind curtain 2."

"Okay, great. Thanks," Kim replied.

"Curtain 2? This ain't 'Let's Make A Deal'," Yolanda said.

"You know this is a small medical center. They don't have a lot of rooms here," Kim pointed out.

Kim led the way down the hall and sure enough behind curtain number 2 was Grandma Effie. She was sitting on the side of the small hospital bed. Her face brightened immediately. "Oh! Look at my grandbabies! Come here and give me a hug!"

The women embraced their grandmother for a moment before Yolanda started flinging questions. "Are you okay? What in the world is going on?"

"Aww, man. I almost had the big one," Grandma Effie said.

"The big one? Grandma Effie, what happened to you?" Kim asked.

"Chile, I ain't talkin' 'bout me. I was talking about on this bingo game I'm playing on my phone. I almost got the big prize. And how did you know I was here?"

"I went by your house and Ms. Bernice said you left on a stretcher."

"I should've known Bernice was gon' tell somebody. She just like an old refrigerator, can't hold nothing."

Kim and Yolanda both laughed as the hovered over Grandma Effie and waited for every word.

"I sprained my ankle when I was working in the yard. I couldn't get up to walk, and since Stanley hadn't made it home, I called 911."

Just hearing Stanley's name made Yolanda feel uneasy.

"Kim, it's good to see you, baby. How your mama doing?"

"She's doing good."

"Well, good. I'm so glad you girls found each other."

"Ain't nothing like having your family," Grandma Effie said, eyeing Yolanda.

"I'm glad you didn't have a real emergency," Kim said.

"Yea, me, too. I'm waiting on my discharge papers now. Stanley went to go see what's taking them so long."

"He's here? Our dad is here?" Kim's eyes lit up like a Christmas tree.

"I'm surprised y'all didn't see him. This hospital ain't that big."

"I'm glad you're okay, Grandma Effie, but I really have to go." Yolanda rambled through her purse and found the $65 she owed. She placed the money in Grandma Effie's hands and turned to leave.

"Don't leave, 'Landa. You can't keep running, baby," Grandma Effie pleaded.

"Yolanda, she's right. Please don't leave." Yolanda heard a man's voice from behind her.

"Stanley, two of your girls are here. Ain't that a blessing? That's Kim."

"I know who she is." Stanley smiled. "She's a grown woman now, but I remember that pretty little face from all the pictures at the house."

"It's nice to meet you." Kim extended her hand to shake, but he pulled her into his arms and hugged her. "Wow, I really do look like you. And Yolanda was right—you two really are twins," she spoke as soon as he released her from his grasp.

"You 'bout to suffocate the girl." Effie laughed.

Stanley stepped back and looked at her again. "Wow! What are you doing with yourself these days?"

"Finishing up my degree in psychology." She grinned.

"I told you, Stanley, she's smart! All your kids are smart!" Grandma Effie added.

Stanley's chest felt broader. "That's amazing. You're all grown up!"

"No thanks to you," Yolanda butted in. She grabbed the back of Kim's jacket and pulled her away from their father. Yolanda twisted Kim's body so that she and Kim were eye-to-eye. She clutched the front panels of Kim's Michael Kors coat. "Hello! Earth to Kim. I cannot believe how you're acting. This man is your deadbeat dad. Are you going to let him off the hook this easily?"

Kim shrugged as though she was unsure of how to respond to Yolanda's words.

Yolanda rolled her eyes. "I'm outta here."

"Wait. Sis, please don't leave," Kim begged.

"You can stay here and act like we one big happy family if you want to but I refuse to let him make a fool out of me," Yolanda spat.

"Yolanda, I want to get to know you. I know I messed up, but let's move past it. Life is too short. Please forgive me," Stanley said with misty eyes.

"Wow. How long did you practice this little Easter speech?" she sassed.

"Just hear him out," Kim suggested.

"Hear him out? For what, Kim? What could he possibly have to say to make up for dropping off the face of the earth and then having the nerve to reappear like he hasn't been gone for thirty years?"

CHAPTER 9

Only seconds ago, Stanley had tried to breathe in all twenty-something years of Kim's life in one big breath. The way her hair was styled, the scent of her perfume, even the quality of her coat's fabric said she had been well taken care of. All of his mother's pictures of Kim at the house didn't do her justice.

Kim's attitude was refreshing, but Yolanda was still as cold as the day she'd nearly run over his foot leaving Effie's house.

Kim stepped aside as Stanley approached Yolanda cautiously. "I know I have a lot of explaining—"

"Really?" Yolanda's head whipped to the side as she cut him off.

Stanley zipped his lips. For as many times as Stanley had been cussed out, had his tires slashed, and had his clothes bleached, he had never seen a woman look at him with this level of animosity. He understood why a woman would be mad about cheating and lying—things he had done *to* them. But how someone could be this mad about what he *hadn't* done was still a mystery to him.

"You can stay here and fall for this act if you want to but I refuse to participate in this circus show." She turned to leave.

"Baby, don't go." Mama Effie hissed.

Kim pulled Yolanda's arm. "Wait, Yolanda. Please don't leave."

With Kim standing between him and Yolanda, Stanley felt safe to speak again. "Yolanda, I want to be here for you and your kids. I know I messed up, but that's in the past. We can start over. Fresh."

"I don't need you and my kids don't need you. Stay away from us," Yolanda yelled.

"Yolanda, just for the record. Calm down and hear him out," Kim said.

"Hear him out? For what, Kim? Whatever he has to say I'm sure it's a lie."

Mama Effie interjected, "He might say some words you been needin' to hear all your life, baby."

"No disrespect, Grandma Effie, but whatever he," she pointed at Stanley, "had to say should have been said thirty years ago. You all go on with the family reunion."

This time, there was no stopping her.

Stanley bit his bottom lip. Felt the tears stinging in his eyes.

Kim balled her fists. "I'm gonna go talk to her."

"Okay. Yeah, yeah. But are you coming back?" Stanley asked.

"Yeah. Sure."

"Okay."

At least he had one daughter on his side.

Grandma Effie tsked.

"What, Momma?"

"That gal's got a right to be mad. You can't just walk into somebody's life and expect them to be all honky-dory about seeing you. Ain't no tellin' how many nights she cried herself to sleep wonderin' why her daddy didn't care nothin' to come see her."

Stanley crossed his arms. *Women.* Why couldn't they just get over stuff and move forward—focus on the future. Forgive and forget. Why did they always insist on dredging through the past? What good did that ever do?

"I done tried my best to let them know that somebody from the Brown side of the family was thinkin' about them as much as I could. But they *your* children, Stanley. And you a different man now, from what I can see. You gotta make 'em see who you are."

"But Yolanda doesn't want to—"

Effie held up a crooked, arthritic finger. "Don't you dare blame her for her pain. You part of the reason she got the pain."

"Kim seems to be fine." Stanley tried again.

"You can't compare one person's heart to another. Some people's hearts got more bumps and bruises on 'em than others. It ain't your place to say how she *should* feel."

Stanley shook his head. "I'll keep trying, Mama."

Grandma Effie sighed. "Well, you've met two. You got one more to go, but you got to handle that one yourself."

CHAPTER 10

Yolanda fumbled for her keys and dropped her purse in the hospital's hallway.

With tears in her eyes, she fell on her knees to retrieve the contents of her purse.

"Sis, let me help you." Kim kneeled down beside her.

"Just please leave me alone." Yolanda snatched up her belongings and stuffed them into the fake leather bag.

"Why are you so angry?" Kim grabbed a tube of lipstick and offered it to Yolanda.

"I can't believe you're asking me that. How can you act like this dude gets the dad of the year award?"

"I never said that. I just think in order for you to heal you have to deal with the issue first."

"I'm healed. My life was fine until he showed up and tore off the scab," Yolanda said as she stood up.

"If you were really healed, fresh skin would have grown over the wound already. You wouldn't be so angry because the area is still sensitive."

"Well thank you Oprah Winfrey *and* Dr. Oz."

"Why are you upset with me? I'm just trying to help."

"Help? Help me how? That's just it, Kim, I don't need your help. You're walking around here hugging the man like you been knowing him forever. He signed over his rights to you for God's sake. If that ain't a punch in the face, I don't know what is. What else do you need him to do? Do you want him to slap a stamp on you that says return to sender?" She hissed.

"Now see, that was just ugly. You didn't have to go there. You can't get upset with me for how I handle our father. I'm personally glad that he decided to give me up, because clearly he wasn't ready to be a father at the time," Kim said, pacing back and forth. "Why can't you understand that, Yolanda?"

"I can't understand it because I have three kids," Yolanda said, holding up a finger for each one. "They are my flesh and blood. It takes a sick person to abandon what's theirs."

"Maybe that's it, Yolanda. Maybe he *was* sick," Kim said.

"He wasn't too sick. He had three more kids. Takes some strength and energy to make babies, you know."

"I don't mean physically sick. Mentally sick. Emotionally sick."

Yolanda shook her head. "You and these psychology classes. Stop making excuses for him. He was wrong. Dead wrong. And he might as well be dead to me now."

"Everyone deserves a second—"

"Kim, you're only saying this because you *have* a Daddy. You grew up with nice things." Yolanda swept her arm up and down, noting Kim's clothes. "You grew up with all the support you needed. You've never had to worry about what you're going to eat. You've never had to worry about who you're going to stay with. You've never stayed in the projects. You didn't have a hard life like I did," Yolanda yelled.

"Life is about choices and it's not my fault that my mother made different choices."

"Ooooooh, so you think just because your mama married a man with some money, that makes you better? You've always thought you were better than me. Just because you live in the suburbs, live in a mini mansion, go to college, and drive a new car don't make you better than me."

"I never said I was better than you, Yolanda. You're putting words in my mouth."

"You said your mother made better choices, that's just like saying your mother was better than mine."

"This has nothing to do with whose life is better. This is about forgiving our father. I don't hold grudges. We have to forgive so that God can forgive us."

"Forgive me for what? Me and God good," she shouted.

"Excuse me, is there a problem?" The hospital security officer arrived on the scene and asked. The officer was slightly overweight and wore a light blue shirt with three missing buttons. The buttons weren't the only thing missing; he also had a few missing teeth. "I need you two ladies to either lower your voices or leave the building now."

"Not a problem. I was leaving anyway," Yolanda announced and walked down the hall and out the door.

Kim's got some nerve trying to tell me what I should do. I don't need him and I don't need her. Yolanda vented to herself as she made the drive back home.

Her cell phone buzzed. Kim's name flashed on the screen.

Yolanda ignored the call and turned her radio up to help her mind transition back into mother-mode. Once again, she had to stuff the emotional events of the day deep down inside because there was work to be done. Three kids to tend to. Gwen would pitch a fit that it had taken Yolanda so long to get home from work.

Yolanda decided that the best thing to do would be to bring home a pizza so her mother wouldn't have to cook. Against her better judgment, she sent her mother a text while driving to let her know about the pizza, then she threw her phone back into her purse.

I bet Kim eats out every chance she gets. Must be nice.

The parking lot at Bab Street Pizza was full. The staff at Bab's was known for putting on a show for its guest. Yolanda watched as they tossed the dough in the air and sang their welcome song.

A man and his three children—two sons and a daughter—caught Yolanda's attention.

"Dad, can we get a booth?" one asked.

"I want money for the arcade," the other said.

"Daddy, can I have some cinnamon sticks?" the little girl asked.

"Anything for you, baby girl," he said and gave her a big hug.

The man smiled and gave both his sons money and went to the booth.

Yolanda wished her children had a relationship with Jesse so they, too, could experience the joy of having a father around. She stared at the family in amazement. Just watching the man interact with his children made her teary.

"Ma'am, how can I help you today?" the cashier asked, bringing Yolanda back to reality.

She ordered a large meat lover's pizza for Deontae and Eric to share and a half pepperoni half sausage for her, Zoey, and Gwen. She took her ticket and sat across from the family. She pretended to be scrolling through her phone while she listened to their conversation. The children's father had asked about their grades and their school friends. He was genuinely concerned about them. Yolanda had never experienced or seen anything like this other than on TV.

When the cashier announced that her order was ready, Yolanda grabbed her pizzas and took one final glance at the family again.

"One day this will be my children," she whispered to herself.

When Yolanda arrived home, Deontae was sitting on the porch. Juggling the pizza boxes and her purse, she got out of the car.

"D, come help your mom out," she said, handing him one of the pizzas.

Deontae grabbed the pizza box but didn't say a word.

"Is there something wrong?" she asked.

"I really need to talk to you about something that happened at school."

"Don't tell me you got suspended for fighting."

"No, ma'am. Can we just talk? Just me and you. Without Granny?" Deontae said with a shaky voice.

"Of course we can, baby. Let me put these pizzas on the table. I'll be right back."

Yolanda took the pizza box back from Deontae, ran in the house, and placed them on the table. She knew Gwen would be in her bedroom doing her Friday night routine—eating chips and salsa and watching her favorite sitcom, "Good Times". She acted as if the Evans family was her family.

Yolanda called to whoever might be listening, "Pizza in the kitchen!" Then she quickly went back outside and sat next to her son on the porch. "Alright. What's on your mind?"

"We're having a football banquet and all of my friends are bringing their dads."

Yolanda sighed.

"Mom, I know you said Dad's working overseas but can you *please* call him so I can talk to him? Please, Mom, please," he begged. "My friend Jacob said he talks to his dad in Germany all the time, and he's been home twice. I want to talk to my dad. Maybe he can come home, too." Deontae placed his head on her shoulder and sobbed like a baby.

Yolanda couldn't find the words to say to Deontae. She knew that, eventually, she'd have to tell him the truth. Looked like "eventually" was today.

She pulled him into her arms and held him tight. Yolanda had never seen this side of her son. She was so used to him acting like a little man.

She had no clue where Jesse even lived, and the last phone number she had for him was from several years ago. The only choice she had was to go to his mother's house and see if she would help her reach out to Jesse. She didn't even know if that would actually work, but somehow, some way, she had to contact him. Not just for Deontae, but for Eric and Zoey, too.

CHAPTER 11

S tanley positioned the phone in the crook of his neck and took a moment to wipe his sweaty hands on his jeans. The phone rang. In a way, he almost wished no one would answer. He wished the cell phone number listed for a real estate agent named Valerie Reyes-Newsome belonged to a different Valerie Reyes-Newsome than the one he'd impregnated, but he knew the odds were against him on that one.

He held onto the phone now. Crossed his arms.

The phone rang again. Now he hoped someone did answer because he didn't want to leave a message. He couldn't just say, "Hey, Valerie, it's Sabrina's dad. Call me back," like a normal father would.

"Hello?" A female voice suddenly interrupted the third ring. Stanley was quite happy. This voice was far too young to be Valerie. He had the wrong number, after all.

"Hi. Um. I'm calling for Valerie Reyes-Newsome?"

"Oh, yeah. This is her number, but her number has been forwarded to my phone because hers is in the shop. I'm her daughter, Sabrina. I can get her for you. May I say who's calling?"

"Did you say you're Sabrina...Brown?" Stanley asked.

"Yes. Who is this?"

"Stanley. Brown."

"Oh," the girl chirped. "Are we related?"

"Yes. I'm your father," Stanley said.

"Oh. Wow. Well. Okay. I guess." She slowly replied.

Stanley laughed nervously. "I know, right?"

"Yeah," she agreed.

Stanley wasn't sure where to start, but given Yolanda's reaction to his sudden appearance, he thought he'd better get to talking pretty quickly. "Let me first say that I'm so sorry I haven't been in your life. There's no excuse for why I haven't been in touch."

He heard Sabrina whispering.

"Hello?" Stanley said after a short pause on the line.

"Is this Stanley Brown?" another voice asked him. "Stanley David Brown?"

It took him a moment to be sure. It was Valerie. Sabrina's mother.

"Yes, Valerie. It's me."

"I knew it was you sniffin' around." She giggled. "My sister-in-law said somebody was asking about me at her job. Was that you?"

"No," Stanley said.

"Oh. Well, how have you been?" Valerie asked.

"I'm good. You?"

"Good. Just working every day, you know."

"Same here. God is good. Could you please put Sabrina back on the phone?"

"Sure thing. She's sitting here smiling. Like she's been missing you all her life."

"She has. And I owe her a lot," Stanley admitted. "I owe you an apology, too, Valerie. I wasn't ready to man up to my responsibilities. You took over my role all by yourself, and that wasn't fair to you or Sabrina. But I'm a different person now. At least I'm trying to be, anyway."

"Wow," Valerie exclaimed. "You *are* a different person. The old Stanley would never admit to being wrong about anything back in the day."

"Thank you, Valerie."

"Your momma still mean and evil?" Valerie asked with a chuckle.

Stanley had almost forgotten how Valerie felt about his mother. This was the reason why Grandma Effie hadn't been able to keep ties with Sabrina. There was nothing but bad blood between Effie and Valerie. The one time Stanley showed his mother a picture of him and Valerie on a cruise ship, she had said that Valerie dressed like a street walker. And then there was the time he'd brought Valerie over for Thanksgiving Dinner and Effie blamed Valerie for stealing Stanley away from Rhonda. That night, Valerie had called Effie an "old hag on a ventilator" who couldn't kiss a man if she wanted to, let alone satisfy him. Things went all the way downhill from there.

Stanley answered Valerie's question. "Momma's still Momma, if that's what you're asking."

"Okay, then. Here's Sabrina again."

More whispering transpired between mother and daughter, but Stanley wasn't able to make out their words.

"Um...so... are you...in town?" Sabrina asked.

"I'm not far," Stanley said.

"Would you like to meet? I mean, I'm really not much for talking on the phone. I'm a texter. And, honestly, I won't believe it's really you until I see you."

"I'd love to meet. Thank you for making the offer."

Stanley and Sabrina ended the call after making plans. She gave him her direct number to confirm.

He wasn't sure if Sabrina was suppressing anger, suspending judgment, or if she just didn't care one way or the other. He'd have to look into her eyes to know for sure.

Sabrina was in disbelief. In just a few hours, she'd be meeting her father. She'd often dreamed of meeting him but didn't know what to expect. *Was he nice? Was he mean? Was he married?* All of these questions ran through her mind.

Sabrina didn't know much about Stanley, only what Valerie told her. Stanley was Valerie's first love. Valerie met him at her job and the two became fast friends. It started off with Valerie sharing her lunch with Stanley every day. The two had been labeled as a couple because they not only hung out at lunch but Valerie also was giving Stanley a ride home every day. Stanley finally asked her out on a date and after dating for a few months she allowed him to move in. According to Valerie they'd lived together for two years and when Valerie told Stanley that she was pregnant, he moved. No notice, no letter, nothing. He just left.

"Sabrina, how do I look?" Valerie came into the living room dressed in a red wrapped dress with a split that was revealing way too much.

"Mom, what are you doing? Why are you dressed like that?"

"I don't want Stanley to see me looking any kind of way."

"He's not coming to see you, he's coming to see me. I honestly don't understand why you're so excited about seeing him. He broke your heart, remember?"

"That was a long time ago and he seems to be a changed man." She adjusted her dress in the mirror.

"How can you tell from one short phone conversation?"

"Something in my heart tells me that he's different," Valerie said with a glow on her face.

"I just don't want you getting your hopes up." Sabrina kissed her on the cheek.

"I'm not getting my hopes up. I'm just excited for you, that's all."

"So explain to me why you cooked so much food?" she asked, walking into the kitchen.

"You can't invite someone over and don't have food, Sabrina."

"We could have had pizza or ordered Chinese." She tried to stick her finger in the chocolate cake but Valerie slapped it away.

Valerie had gone all out for Stanley. Along with the chocolate cake for dessert, she cooked his old favorite meal—smothered pork chops, garlic mashed potatoes, corn on the cobb, salad, and sweet tea.

The doorbell rang and both Sabrina and Valerie went to answer it.

Sabrina sighed loudly. Valerie stepped back. Sabrina opened the door and Stanley was standing there with a huge smile and a bouquet of multicolored flowers.

"Hey, Stanley come on in," Valerie said, hugging him. She eyed the flowers. "These are beautiful!"

"Thank you." Stanley turned his attention to Sabrina. "They're for you."

"Thank you." Sabrina took the flowers from him.

"You still looking good, Stanley," Valerie blurted out.

The room went silent for a brief moment.

"Well, have a seat." Valerie ushered him to the couch.

Sabrina placed the flowers in a vase and joined them in the living room. She sat on the love seat across from her mother and Stanley, who were sitting on the sofa.

"Thanks again for the flowers. They're beautiful."

"You're welcome, sweetheart."

"I'm sorry, I don't know what I should call you."

"Call me whatever you feel comfortable calling me." Stanley smiled.

"I'm comfortable with calling you Stanley, I guess," Sabrina said shyly. "Is that okay?"

"Works for me. But I do hope to earn the title of father one of these days."

Sabrina nodded. "Fair enough. Since we're both being so blunt, can you tell me why you decided to look me up?"

Stanley nodded eagerly. "I've turned over a new leaf in life, and it's time that I do right by you."

"So you're a changed man for real?" Valerie beamed, scooting closer to him.

"I'm a work in progress," Stanley stated.

"Have you been in contact with my sisters? Granda Effie told me about them and I'd love to one day meet them, too," Sabrina said.

"I've briefly been in contact with them."

"Do you have a wife or a girlfriend?" Valerie quizzed him.

"I'm single," Stanley replied.

"Do you have any pictures of my sisters?" Sabrina gave her mother a side-eye.

"No I don't have any pictures of them but I know that they are both on Facebook."

"I'm on Facebook, too. Tell me their names so that I can look them up."

"Yolanda Brown and Kim Maxwell are their names."

Sabrina retrieved her phone from the pocket of her jeans and looked up her sisters. Although there were several profiles that popped up, she knew which one belonged to her sisters. They all shared the same eye color and they all looked just like Stanley. Sabrina starred at her phone, astonished because Kim was her twin.

"Mom, look at this picture."

Valerie took the phone. "That's a beautiful picture of you. When did you take this?"

"That's not me, that's Kim."

"Lord, y'all look so much alike. Yep, she's definitely your sister."

"All of you look alike," Stanley added with a smile.

Valerie returned the phone to Sabrina. "I cooked dinner, Stanley. Made all your favorites, just like the old days. I hope you're hungry. I'll make you a plate." Valerie sped off to the kitchen before he could answer.

Finally alone with her father, Sabrina said, "I'm glad you took the time to find me."

"Me, too." His eyes seemed to become misty. "Where's the bathroom?" he asked.

Sabrina pointed him to the bathroom. Stanley followed her directions. Then, Sabrina went into the kitchen with Valerie.

"Mom, remember, don't get your hopes up too high," she warned her.

"He's single, I'm single. Who knows what could happen?" Valerie chirped.

When Stanley came out of the restroom, Valerie escorted him to the dining room table. They ate dinner as Sabrina caught him up on what was taking place in her life. She told him that she'd had only been out of high school for a few years and was now attending community college taking her basics. "I'm taking twelve hours a semester. Not too fast," Sabrina said. "I earned several scholarships, but those books can bite a hole in the budget." She giggled.

"Yes," Stanley agreed. "I remember how expensive books were when I was in college. I can't imagine how much they cost now."

Stanley told Sabrina that he was living with his mother, taking care of her and that he would tell her sisters about her. He also stated that he wanted them to all get together soon.

Valerie spent the evening gazing into Stanley's eyes, trying to see if there was still a spark there. Unfortunately Stanley hadn't really paid her too much attention, his focus really was on Sabrina. Stanley gave Sabrina $100. "For books." He winked at her.

"Thank you," she said, stuffing the twenties into her pocket.

"It's my pleasure. I'll be in touch again real soon." Stanley hugged Sabrina and left.

"Tonight was perfect. I'm so glad I got a chance to meet my dad." Sabrina smiled.

"I just wish he would have stayed longer," Valerie whined.

"Mom, you're making this about you. Dad said he had to get going so that he could be ready for church tomorrow. Why are you smiling at me like that?" Sabrina asked.

"You just called him Dad." Valerie smiled.

"Umm, I guess I did. It just rolled off my tongue." Sabrina felt herself getting emotional.

"It's okay. He's your dad and you have every right to call him that."

"I'm just glad I have a chance to get to know him."

"Me, too, baby. Me, too," she said, hugging her.

CHAPTER 12

"Mom, I have something to talk to you about," Kim said as she and her mother, Sherry, prepared dinner. "What's going on? Is there something wrong?" Sherry buttered the rolls and placed them in the oven.

"Well, I saw my dad the other day and he wants to have lunch with me," she said with hesitation.

"Excuse me, who did you say you saw?" Sherry said with a major attitude.

"I saw my dad. Stanley."

"That's what I thought you said. When did all this happen?" she sassed.

"When I went to the hospital to see Grandma Effie. He was there."

"And so now he wants to have lunch? Let me guess, he needs a kidney or liver and he thinks you're a match," Sherry spat.

"Mom, no. Now you're being dramatic. It's not like that at all." Kim sighed.

"How do you know?"

"He says he's a changed man."

"The only thing he's good at changing is addresses," Sherry said matter-of-factly.

"Mom, you're judging him. All my life you've told me not to judge people and to give people a fair chance," Kim pointed out.

"He doesn't *deserve* a chance." Sherry raised her voice.

"Now you sound just like Yolanda."

Sherry's brows knit. "That's his oldest daughter, right?"

70

Kim nodded.

"What does Yolanda have to do with this?"

"She wants nothing to do with him. She won't give him a chance to talk or anything."

"Well, at least somebody has some sense," Sherry said and sat down at the table.

"Who has sense?" Larry asked as he joined Sherry at the kitchen table and kissed her cheek.

"Do you want me to tell him, or do you want to tell him?" Sherry asked.

"Tell me what?" Larry searched Sherry's face for clues. Sherry's eyes were fixed on Kim.

Kim swallowed hard. "The other day I saw my dad and he wants to have lunch with me tomorrow."

"So let me get this straight. You saw Stanley and he all of a sudden wants to have lunch with you? Why am I just now finding out about this?" Larry looked at Sherry.

"Don't look at me. I just found out today, too."

"Kim, aren't you the least bit suspicious about him wanting to meet up with you now? I mean, the man gave up his parental rights for God's sake," Larry yelled.

"Mom and Dad, I know you are both concerned, but I really think Stanley is a changed man. I want to hear him out and see what he has to say."

"You mean see what he needs. He's always been selfish and knowing him like I do I know, he's up to no good."

"You haven't seen him in years, and you're not being fair."

"Fair? You want me to be fair towards a man who didn't care enough about you to stay in your life? And now you want me to roll out a welcome mat for him. I don't think so," Sherry shouted.

"Mom, I respect you and I respect your opinion, but I don't need your permission to have lunch with him," Kim said sternly.

"Permission. Oh, so since you about to be thirty you think

you can just make a decision that will affect your family and we're supposed to just be quiet about it?" Larry slammed his fist on the table.

"I don't mean to upset you guys, but I'm having lunch with Stanley. I have every right to do it because at the end of the day he is family, too." Kim took the rolls out of the oven and placed them on the counter to cool off.

"Family, Umph the only family you have is right here," Sherry sassed.

"Kim, just think about the consequences. What if he does something to hurt you?" Larry pointed out.

"I know you mean well, Dad, and I know you want to protect me. I promise you, there's nothing to worry about. I don't think Stanley will do anything to hurt me."

"Kim, clearly he's already fooled you. Open your eyes, baby girl. This is one of his schemes. He wants something. I don't know what it is, but I know it's *something*," Sherry said with tears in her eyes.

"Mom, please, just trust me on this." Kim walked over to her mom and hugged her.

"I trust you. It's him I'm having issues with," she pointed out.

"I don't trust him and I don't want you around him," Larry said and walked out of the kitchen.

After that night, Kim had decided not to tell her parents any more about the upcoming meeting with Stanley. Her parents had always been overprotective. They hadn't wanted her to play sports because she might get hurt. They hadn't wanted her to venture too far off for college because they never wanted her to feel alone. There was no doubt that Sherry and Larry loved her, but if they had their way, she'd still be living at home with a 10:00 p.m. curfew. Sooner or later, they would have to trust that they had raised Kim right and that she was capable of making sound decisions.

Moving into an apartment with her high school friend, Arisha, had been a struggle financially, but Kim was glad she'd made that decision. Working as a substitute and attending college didn't bring in much money, but Kim was proud of herself for stepping out on faith and giving herself a chance to grow up. Knowing that her parents were always in her corner was comforting. But even more comforting was the fact that she was learning to depend on God for everything, from long-term substitute assignments, which paid more, as well as scholarships to help cover tuition expenses. She and God had an ongoing joke—when she earned her next degree, she would write His name underneath hers on the certificate because she certainly couldn't have earned it without Him.

This newfound confidence was what gave her the ability to explore the relationship with Stanley all the more. Kim was praying that maybe Yolanda could come to forgive their father, too. Maybe Yolanda and Stanley would never have a traditional father-daughter relationship, but if Yolanda could at least forgive him, she wouldn't keep poisoning herself with anger.

Kim pulled into the closest parking spot in the shopping center's parking lot. She and Stanley had agreed to meet at the coffee shop inside a local bookstore. She had spent many hours there studying and reading in previous semesters. For a mom-and-pop store, it was quite busy, but there were some quiet nooks and corners to be had by those who knew the shop well.

Since she was early, Kim waited on a couch for her father to arrive. She slid the latest edition of *Essence* from the magazine rack and browsed through the articles.

Five minutes passed. Still no Stanley.

Seven minutes. Maybe my mother was right. *Maybe Stanley is still the same selfish man he's always been. Lord, I need you to show me.*

As Kim continued to flip through the magazine, one article about black women in education caught her attention and she became so engrossed in the information that she'd nearly jumped when Stanley said, "Hello, Kim."

"Oh! Hello." She folded the magazine and stood to hug him.

"Sorry I'm a little late. There was a car accident on my route here."

"No worries. I was just reading," Kim said.

"A book worm, huh?"

"I guess you could say that."

"You're just like your mom. Brilliant." Stanley smiled.

"Awww, thanks." Kim whipped her phone from her pocket. Now was her chance to see if her mother's fears were feasible. "We should take the booth in the back." She pointed toward the rear of the building that had once been a house. "Could you excuse me for a second? I need to use the ladies' room."

"Sure thing," Stanley said. "Don't leave me hanging, now."

"Anyway," Kim joked.

As soon as Stanley turned around to go to the booth, Kim stepped toward the ladies' room and opened a traffic app on her phone. Sure enough, there was a red line and a starburst on the highway between their towns. Her father hadn't been lying. He really was late by no fault of his own.

Kim breathed a sigh of relief and thanked God for this little confirmation.

Stanley waited patiently for Kim to return from the restroom. He surveyed the bookstore. Shelves and shelves of literature gave the building a stale paper smell underneath the aroma of roasted coffee beans. The areas between shelves were covered with posters of celebrities reading. Old fashioned wallpaper peeked between the shelves and the posters. He could see why people like Kim would enjoy this place.

He looked around at the other patrons in the bookstore. Most appeared to be college kids, varied ethnicities, probably clueless about the struggles of their respective ancestors. The nerdy types with iPhones and sporting tiny tattoos that their parents probably didn't know about. These were the kinds of kids who had it made and didn't even know it.

Thank You, Lord, for watching over my daughter.

Back when he was in college, he had envied these types. They could call home and ask Mom and Dad for whatever they needed and their parents would be there for them. Not so with Stanley. His mother couldn't afford to send him anything, not that he would have asked her anyway. Eighteen was a magic number. He'd always thought of these kids whose parents continued to support them after eighteen as weaklings who couldn't fare for themselves. They'd be eaten alive by life as soon as the first problem hit. They were doomed for failure.

Or at least that's what he told himself to keep from wondering why his mother wouldn't so much as send him a bar of soap if he needed it. Not to mention his own father. Richmond Warren. The entire Warren family had more than enough money to send Stanley something while he was in college. But that was neither here nor there. The Warrens had nothing to do with Stanley, and he didn't want to deal with them, either. His father had washed his hands of them a long time ago and, according to Mama Effie, it was for the best. Some things needed to stay in the past. Stanley had never questioned it. Never thought twice about it. Didn't overanalyze it. Life went on.

"Sorry about that," Kim said as she took a seat across from him.

"No problem. This is a nice place." He was proud that his daughter was amongst this privileged group. The fact that she was so successful actually made Stanley feel as though he had done the best thing for Kim by relinquishing his parental rights. He couldn't have ever given Kim all the things her mother and adopted father had. *It was probably best that I exited the picture when I did.*

But now that he was back, Stanley's only hope was that he

could somehow add to Kim's life. If he could get his girls back on track, he could finally be the man he always hoped he would someday be.

"This house was built in the 1940's," Kim informed him. "The owner died and left it to the library. The library sold it to a private owner, who kept a lot of the books. There was a big lawsuit and everything. Lots of history here."

"Interesting." Stanley nodded. His daughter's zest for information made him laugh inside. This girl was going to be so much fun.

"I ordered us both hot chocolate. Is that okay?"

"Yes, but you should have allowed me to pay for it," Stanley said. "It's the least I can do."

"It's okay," Kim said. She slung her purse on the empty space next to her. "So. What's on your mind?"

"I was going to ask you the same thing."

"Okay. Well, I don't want to be rude. And I don't blame you for anything. I'm not mad. I never wanted for anything—money, love, a dad. I just want to know why you made the decision not to be a part of my earlier years."

Stanley liked the way she said that—her *earlier* years. There were middle years and later years to come, hopefully, and he wanted to be there for those years indeed. Stanley cleared his throat. "I left because I was in a bad place. I wasn't ready to be a father. I was drinking a lot, partying, making a lot of stupid decisions, couldn't keep a job."

"Got caught up with the wrong crowd?" Kim asked sympathetically.

"No, I didn't get *caught up* with the wrong crowd, I *was* the wrong crowd," Stanley admitted to his daughter. "Talked a lot of people—mostly women—into bad situations. Selfish and self-destructive all at the same time."

"Alrighty then." Kim pursed her lips.

"But God," Stanley added. "And now that I see the young

woman you've turned out to be, I see I missed out on a lot. And I'm sorry. But a part of me feels like you didn't need me speaking a lot of negativity and my womanizing thoughts into your head anyway. Now you don't have to unlearn my foolishness."

Kim poked out her lips. Tilted her head to the side. "Hmph."

"What?" Stanley probed.

"So, you know I'm taking psychology classes, right?"

He nodded.

She squinted her eyes as though a sudden, tiny revelation had appeared in the distance. "I'm learning more and more how important a parent's words are in a child's life. And if what you're telling me is that you were so messed up, so out there, so destructive to yourself back in your younger days...I don't know. It's almost like you being away from me was the mercy of God. 'Cause like, whatever it was that was in you at the time, whatever demons you were wrestling with at the time that caused you to make destructive decisions, I certainly didn't need them speaking into my life as well."

Stanley's mouth fell open. "Wow."

Kim continued. "Plus, I believe the Bible, that all things work together for good to those who love God and are called according to His purposes. I don't think it was a good thing for you to not be in my life, but I believe God *worked it* for His good."

"Romans eight and twenty-eight," Stanley said with a smile. He'd learned this verse in the men's fellowship.

"Yes," Kim agreed. "This is what I live by. It's gotten me this far. I think it'll take me on through life."

"You're so blessed, Kim, to have this kind of revelation so young in life. If I'd had it sooner, I wouldn't have made such a mess of things," Stanley admitted.

Kim put her hand on his. "It's never too late to start believing in God's word."

Her touch melted Stanley's heart. He knew that Kim wasn't

angry, but he hadn't realized that she was actually so whole that she could even help him. "Thank you, Kim."

They spent an hour catching up on thirty years. Kim's phone was filled with pictures of her family and friends and scenes from her life that showed how happy and full her life was. From praise dancing to spelling bee championships to scholarships, his daughter was quite the overachiever.

Stanley's chest seemed to swell with every story told, every laugh, every recollection of Kim's awards and recognitions, especially her faith in the Lord. Being in Kim's life would definitely give him another reason to become the best man he could be.

When Kim asked Stanley about the last thirty years of his life, he summed it up with, "Not nearly as exciting as yours."

She laughed. "Oh come on. Surely you've done something you're proud of."

He shook his head. Shrugged. "No. I can't think of anything. You heard that song 'Poppa was a rolling stone'?"

"Yeah."

"That was me. No place to call my own. Just living from pillar to post. Trying to survive. Nothing worth repeating until last year when I received Christ. Started going to church, studying the Word, hanging with a different crowd. Moved back home to take care of my mother because my sister, your Aunt, had to move out of town. Trying to become a Deacon at Warren Grove Baptist Church."

Kim's bright eyes flashed with excitement. "That's wonderful. You must be so grateful."

"I am."

"So, how are my other siblings? Sabrina, right? And isn't there a boy? I think Grandma Effie said something about him a few times."

"Sabrina's fine. Of course you already know Yolanda. But I'm sorry to tell you... your brother recently passed. Todderick."

Shock painted her face. "Oh my gosh. What happened?"

"Hanging with the wrong crowd, according to his mother. I really don't know. His death is part of what drove me to connect with you and your sisters. I don't want to get another obituary for one of my kids in the mail."

"What?!You found out through the mail? That's worse than finding out online."

"I know, right?"

"You must have really made his mother angry."

"I've made a lot of people angry," Stanley admitted. "I want to do just the opposite from now on."

"Well, let's keep it going. How about we make some new memories together? Some stuff you'll want to keep in mind forever. Why don't you come to my birthday party? My mom and dad will be there and we can all start a new chapter. What do you say?"

Kim optimistic attitude was easy to love. How could he say no? "I wouldn't miss it for the world."

CHAPTER 13

The fast song the choir sang seemed to get all in his feet. Stanley wasn't one to stand up during the choral selections, but he couldn't help himself. Debbie had the entire church bumping in praise. It was hard not to mix his feelings for Debbie with his worship of the Lord. Both were a blessing, even if Debbie didn't know it.

Pastor Roundtree's message, based on Romans 12:18, about keeping peace so long as it was in your power was right on time, too. He was doing everything within his power to right wrongs. *Thank You, Lord.*

After service, Deacon Lewis approached Stanley. "Brother Brown, how are you?"

"I'm good. You?"

"Never been better." He pulled Stanley to the side, out of the exiting flow of traffic. "I want you to know that I was able to get to the bottom of that situation last week. You were right. Someone did talk. We've taken disciplinary action. On behalf of the Deacon's board, I do apologize. That's not what we're about."

"Thank you. I appreciate you letting me know."

"And we are still prayerfully considering you. We'll let you know as soon as a decision is made."

The men shook hands.

"Thank you. I look forward to hearing from you," Stanley said.

Stanley was excited again about the possibility of becoming a deacon, a trusted leader in the church. He took a deep breath and, emboldened by this news, decided now was as good a time as any to let Debbie know that the church still believed in him, and maybe she should, too.

Without thinking too much about it, Stanley met Debbie at her car, which he remembered vividly from their last conversation. "Morning, Debbie."

"Morning, Brother Brown," she said dryly.

"Wondering if I could have a moment of your time."

Debbie looked around nervously. "I already told you, you need to—"

"I heard you. You're right. And I'm doing something about it," Stanley said. He shoved his hands into his pockets to hide the fidgeting. He'd rarely been in this position, waiting for a woman to decide if he was worth her time. His relationships were usually the other way around.

"Are you really making an effort to reconnect with your children?"

"Yes, I am," he stated. "But I still have to eat in between my efforts. I'd enjoy your company."

A smile broke out on her face, and Stanley breathed again.

"Follow me," Debbie said.

Stanley didn't even ask where she was going because it didn't matter. He'd follow that pretty face and sweet voice anywhere.

Stanley's truck didn't have as much get-up-and-go as Debbie's vehicle. He lost her a few times on the freeway. She was probably slowing down so that he could keep up. Stanley recalled the time he had driven a brand new Corvette. It had belonged to his girlfriend at the time, a woman named Elvira. She was a high-up with the Federal Emergency Management Agency and was often called to travel to emergencies all over the country, which meant Stanley was left behind to manage her home and two dogs when she was gone. He enjoyed the arrangement, actually. When Elvira was gone, he had access to the Corvette and he had the four-bedroom house in the suburbs of Dallas all to himself, all bills paid. It got to a point where Stanley watched the weather report in hopes of an impending hurricane.

He'd lost the keys to the sports car and the convenient relationship with Elvira when someone had seen him in the car with another woman and told Elvira about it.

Stanley had a knack for messing good things up. He hoped that he wasn't on the verge of doing the same thing with Debbie now.

He calmed himself with the idea that he was a different man. He wasn't scheming, living from one woman to the next. *I'm a new creature in Christ.*

Debbie exited near a developing city just outside of Warren Grove at the kind of shopping center Kim's type of people would have liked. Starbuck's Coffee, a cupcake place, and some kind of trampoline center. He smiled as he thought of his middle daughter and her sweet demeanor.

Debbie parked in front of an ice cream parlor. *Ice cream?* They hadn't eaten meat and potatoes yet.

She exited her car and waited for him. Stanley didn't try to hide the confused expression on his face.

"I know, I know. No dessert before dinner. But they have the best protein smoothies. You'll see."

"Protein smoothies?" he questioned. But after stealing another glance at Debbie's figure, he realized he should have known she was a healthy eater.

Stanley told his stomach to behave for the time being as he and Debbie ordered protein-packed strawberry smoothies. Debbie teased him for his reluctance as soon as he took his first gulp and gave the smoothie its due.

He wanted to give Debbie her due, too, but wasn't sure how she would take a compliment of her soft pearls, the way she's swept her hair up into a loose knot, her sweet perfume, and the light makeup she'd used to enhance her already beautiful face. He decided to compliment her on the choice of food instead. "Not bad for something so healthy."

"I told you," she said, taking a seat at a tall circular table with barstools.

Stanley took another sip, savoring the sweetness and imagining his muscles getting bigger by the moment. He'd been told all of his adult life that he could hang a suit well. This shake couldn't hurt.

After a few more sips, the slight aftertaste was gone. "I'll have to get a few more of these."

"Aaah! I knew you'd like it."

Stanley turned on his charm. "So you've been thinking about me?"

His comment caught Debbie mid-slurp. She quickly shook her head as she swallowed. "No. I say that to everyone I bring here."

"Ooh, so you bring all your men here on the first date." Stanley laughed. "You sure know how to cut a brother down."

"Brother Brown, I am—"

"Please. Call me Stanley."

"*Stanley*. I am not trying to cut you down. And I am not in the habit of bringing *all my men* anywhere."

He nodded because she *didn't* say that this wasn't a date.

"Only the last dozen or so men," Debbie said with a smirk.

He was glad to see that Debbie was a terrible liar. "You playin', but you've probably had all kinds of men knocking down your door. A beautiful voice like yours. A nice smile. Good personality. Good peeps."

"What makes you think you know me?" Debbie asked.

How could he explain that Debbie was one of the first women who held him to a standard before he even got her phone number? How could he explain that he knew his usual type and she wasn't it? There was no way to say those things without sounding like he was trying to brag. "Just a feeling I have." He downplayed his thoughts.

"So. I'm interested to know how things are going with your

children."

Stanley tilted his head to the right. "Two out of three seem fine with me. But my oldest daughter's so angry and bitter. It's weird—I mean, I've said I'm sorry. I've told her that I want to move forward. She's just…I don't know what's wrong with her or how to fix it."

Debbie's face went blank. "Really?"

"Yeah, really. She's just—"

"No. I mean you really don't know why she's still angry?"

"I mean…what else can I say except I'm sorry?"

Debbie blinked twice. A strained expression crossed her face. Finally, she said, "Do you have any idea how important a father is in a child's life?"

The question seemed almost silly to Stanley. "Some people have fathers, some don't. You just learn to live with the hand you're dealt. That's how I see it."

Debbie squinted her eyes. "Are you serious?"

"Yeah. I didn't have my father. I never questioned it. If he called me right now and asked me to come have a beer with him, I would. I'd probably have a soda instead of the beer, but I'd go. Listen to the man. And at the end of our conversation, we'd shake hands and move on. If he wanted a relationship, cool. If not, that would be cool, too."

Debbie's eyebrows shot up in disbelief. She shook her head as though snapping out of a dream. "I suppose that's one way to look at it."

"That's the way it *is*," Stanley said. "You can't relive the past. No need in crying over spilled milk. As long as you're still alive, be thankful. Live and let live. No regrets."

"Okay, stop." Debbie held out a hand. "Enough with the clichés." She set her drink on the table. Crossed her arms.

Stanley didn't like the feel of this, but he liked the way Debbie looked at him. From the lines in her forehead, he could tell she was close to being angry, which meant she cared. Maybe not about him, so much, but he was definitely glad to see this passionate side of her.

"I don't want to give you any unsolicited advice, so let me ask you first: Do you want to know why your firstborn is upset with you?"

"Go ahead."

Debbie uncrossed her arms and leaned in. "First of all, kids need all the financial help they can get. I assume that even if you weren't there emotionally, you did the right thing financially?"

Slowly, Stanley shook his head. "Can't say I did."

"Didn't the mothers file for child support?" Debbie questioned.

"Yolanda's mom did, but she didn't really keep up with it so the state didn't really follow up. Plus, I moved out of state for a little while. Stuff just got lost in the paperwork. Sabrina's mom still wanted to get back together, so she didn't file. Kim's stepfather adopted her." He wasn't ready to talk about Todderick yet. "The truth is, I've never really kept a job until now. That's the way my life has gone."

"How did you eat?"

"Friends," he summarized.

Debbie drank the news down with a sip of smoothie. Stanley was glad to see the judgment draining from her face.

"Okay, so the finances are one thing. Secondly, and perhaps most importantly, deep down inside, every little girl wants to be loved, protected, and adored by her father. Some girls learn to quell that feeling and focus on other things. Some girls are blessed with another father who fills that void. Some girls learn to know their Heavenly Father as a father to the fatherless. But some girls have an extremely hard time overlooking that void. They spend their whole lives asking themselves questions like why didn't my father love me? What did I do to make him leave me? And given the right climate, the right circumstances, the enemy uses those questions to strike at her over and over again."

These words horrified Stanley because, as Debbie spoke, it was as though every syllable added another element to the picture forming in his mind's eye. Suddenly, he could envision a little green-eyed girl whose beautiful eyes were filled with tears. Her body was curled in the fetal position, heaving as she cried. Tigers towered over her, growling and bearing their claws, ready to strike at any moment. All the girl could do was grab her sides tighter and hope the tigers wouldn't eat her alive.

Now it was Stanley's turn to snap out of a dream-like state. "You paint a very vivid picture."

"I know it well. I'm the little girl who had to learn to lean on God as my father. My dad didn't leave voluntarily. He died from cancer when I was in fifth grade, but I still felt abandoned and internalized his death as my fault. Didn't make a lick of sense, but that's how the enemy twisted it. Left to my own devices, I would have resorted to self-destructive behavior—drinking, promiscuity, stuffing myself with food."

The list rang a bell with Stanley because he'd been guilty of the first two, though he'd never related it to his own father's absence.

But all this talk about the past was weighing Stanley down. There was nothing he could do about that child who was curled up in a ball. "Yolanda's thirty years old now, though. She's not that same little girl. She has kids. They don't have a father, from what I can tell. She knows by now that things don't always work out the way you planned."

"Did you ever have a plan in the first place, Stanley?"

"A plan for what?"

"A plan to be a father? A plan to be there for your children even if things didn't work out between you and the mother?"

He considered the questions. "Can't say that I did. I never planned to get anybody pregnant in the first place."

"Maybe that's a good excuse for the first child, but by the second and the third, you knew you were plenty fertile, right?"

Stanley didn't like her tone anymore. "Look, I didn't come here for a lecture. I was young back then. I made a lot of mistakes, but I'm trying to do right now."

"You can't do right until you acknowledge the depth of her pain, until you look into her eyes and see what actually happened in her heart."

Stanley threw his hands in the air. "See, this here is one of my pet peeves with females. Why do y'all have to *do* this? Why do you all have to dredge up all these emotions and make everyone feel uncomfortable in order to get closure? Why do you need closure anyway? Closure happens every night when the clock strikes midnight, the start of a new day."

"No, no, no, no, no," Debbie rattled off. "What *you* want is to avoid being uncomfortable. To avoid feeling the way she has felt all this time. It's like she's fallen into a pit and you want to yell down into it and tell her to come out without actually going down in there with her and walking up out of it hand-in-hand. You can't save her without going *down* there to get her."

He leaned back and tried to let Debbie's words soak in. "What if I go into the pit and she doesn't want to come out? Then I'll be down there cryin' with her for nothing. Looking like a fool."

"Stanley, this isn't about you. The goal is not to keep *you* as comfortable as possible or to protect *you* from being vulnerable. You gotta abandon yourself. Let go. Let yourself feel what she's felt for thirty-something years. Learn how to empathize not for the sake of commiserating but in order to let her know that you understand how deeply you hurt her. If she comes out of the pit, wonderful. If she wants to stay there after you've done all you can, that will be her choice. If she decides not to change her mind for another thirty years, it's still her choice. Stop standing on the rim, keeping yourself safe. Your job as her father is to go down there to get your daughter out!"

Somehow, for some reason, Stanley finally understood why Yolanda seemed to hate the ground he walked on. Debbie had done an excellent job of exposing the foundational points of Woman 101.

He was ready to help Yolanda—if she was willing.

CHAPTER 14

Yolanda looked at Kim's invitation again for the third time. Kim was having a semi-formal birthday party at the Struze Hotel. The Struze, with its 100-foot-high domed ceilings, embroidered silk sofas, exquisite paintings, and beautiful marbled floors, was pretty much considered hotel heaven.

The inside of the invitation caught Yolanda's eye. It was trimmed in lace and there was a beautiful photo of Kim in the center wearing a crimson red dress with a string of beautiful pearls.

Look at Lil Miss Bougie, trying to be all grand. She'll probably get Stanley, the father of the year, to walk her in. I won't be attending

Yolanda shook her head and placed the invitation in her bedroom drawer.

She hadn't talked to Kim since their argument at the hospital. She didn't want to think about Kim or Stanley. She knew she needed to call to check on Grandma Effie. She'd been putting it off because she didn't want to have to talk to Stanley if he happened to answer the phone. But she would have felt terrible if she'd received bad news about her grandmother if she waited too much longer to call.

Yolanda slowly dialed the number and whispered a prayer. *Lord, please let Grandma Effie answer. And don't let her ask me about Stanley.*

"Landa, Hey, baby. How you doing?"

"I'm doing great. How are you feeling?"

"Oh, I'm blessed. I won't complain, ain't no need to," she said in a churchy voice.

That was all Yolanda needed to hear. She could end this call now. "Well, good. Glad you're okay. I'll talk to you later, Gran—"

"Wait a minute, slow down. What's your rush?"

"No rush, just got some things to do."

"Well, before you go, I have something that I need to tell you."

"Grandma, can I please just call you back?" She sighed.

"No, you may not. This is something I gotta get off my chest. It'll only take a few minutes. You hear me, Landa?"

Yolanda hesitated to answer. "Yes, ma'am." She braced herself because she knew the conversation was going to be about Stanley.

"Landa, your daddy is doing the best that he can with you."

"How can you take his side?" Yolanda slightly raised her voice.

"Let me finish. Your daddy is doing the best that he can, considering his circumstances. Stanley grew up without his father. His daddy lived right around the corner from him and didn't want nothing to do with him."

"Why didn't you make sure he knew his father, especially since he lived right around the corner?"

"It wasn't that simple." Effie cleared her throat. "You see, Landa, Stanley was born out of an affair I had with his daddy. Back then, it was bad enough having a child out of wedlock. But an affair—folks would rather have a back alley abortion than give birth to such an unwanted child. Stanley's father was an upstanding man in the community. He owned a funeral home and some businesses along with Stanley's uncles. One of his family members even got a doctorate degree. His whole family was one of them black families everybody looked up to—even white people. Stanley's daddy paid me to keep my mouth closed and of course I was young, dumb, and in love so I did what he asked me to."

"Oh, Grandma, that's awful. I'm sorry that happened to you."

"I went through my pregnancy by myself, and when Stanley was born I raised him by myself. He's never had any dealings with Henry Jeffrey Warren or his family."

"Warren? So you didn't name him after his father?" Yolanda asked.

"Back then it was frowned upon if a woman gave her child the last name of a man she wasn't married to. Henry had already threatened to take my home from me, so I had no choice but to give Stanley my last name."

"So, was Henry your landlord?"

"Yes, and his family owned a lot of property in Big Oak. And since I didn't have a pot to pee in or a window to throw it out of, I had no choice." Grandma Effie sniffled.

"Oh Grandma, don't cry. You did what you felt was best," Yolanda said with a soft voice.

"This isn't something I'm proud of, but I felt like if I explained to you how Stanley grew up, then maybe you'd understand him."

"Grandma, no disrespect, but it seems to me that since he grew up fatherless, he shouldn't want his children to be the same way," Yolanda pointed out.

"You can't be what you were never taught to be. Stanley didn't have nobody to tell him or teach him about being a father."

"He could have tried," Yolanda said teary eyed. Her emotions were getting the best of her. This was just too much to process.

"Landa, baby, I know you're upset and rightfully so, but baby, please find it in your heart to forgive him. Forgive him for yourself, so that you won't have bitterness in your heart. The Bible says in Ephesians, 'let all bitterness and wrath and anger and clamor and slander be put away from you, along with all malice. Be kind to one another, tenderhearted, forgiving one another, as God in Christ forgave you.'"

"Grandma Effie, I just don't understand why he disappeared."

"That's 'cause you tryin' to make sense of sin. Sin don't make no sense in the first place. It's just plain wrong. Ain't ever gonna be no excuse good enough to make up for what he did. Never. Your daddy was a stinkin' hot, smokin' mess back then. Woulda drove your momma crazy 'cause he almost drove *me* crazy and I'm his momma.

"But God has been working on Stanley and now that he's changing, he can be the father you need, Landa," Effie pleaded.

"It's too late. I don't need a father. I'm busy trying to raise my own children," Yolanda stated.

"It's never too late, baby. You always need a father, you're never too old," Grandma Effie argued.

"I don't need to be nurtured. I'm a grown woman now."

"You may be grown, but you're never too old to learn from your parents. You ain't through growing up. You still got a long ways to go."

"Grandma Effie, I gotta go."

"I hope you take heed to what I said. I love you, baby."

"Love you, too." Yolanda choked back her tears.

Yolanda disconnected the call and allowed the waterfall of tears to flow. She couldn't believe what Grandma Effie had just told her. She wanted to just blink three times and wake up from what felt like a horrible nightmare. The more she thought about it, it made her realize that this was a cycle. Gwen grew up fatherless, Stanley grew up fatherless, she grew up fatherless, and now her kids were, too. It was up to her to break this cycle. She owed it to Deontae, Eric, and Zoey to at least try to contact Jesse. After all, she'd promised Deontae.

Yolanda scrolled through her Facebook page and located Wanda Moore, Jesse's older sister. She was going to send her a message, but saw that her phone number was listed and decided to call her instead. She hadn't seen or heard from Wanda in years so she didn't know what the outcome would be. With trembling hands, she pushed the call button and waited for the phone to ring.

On the fourth ring Wanda answered the phone.

"Hello…ummm…Wanda, this is Yolanda Brown."

"Yolanda Brown, as in Jesse's baby mama?" Wanda said sarcastically.

"Yolanda Brown as in the *mother* of his children," Yolanda corrected her.

"Whatever. It's all the same. What do you want?" Wanda sassed.

"I was wondering if you could give me a number for Jesse."

"Hump, ain't you a trip? You want a number for my brother? Why now?"

"What do you mean, why now? He's their father and I need to get in contact with him," Yolanda said sharply.

"When he was trying to get in contact with you, your mama said she didn't know how to contact you, and that you didn't need nothing from my brother."

"And just when did this take place?" Yolanda snapped.

"Look, I just know that's what Jesse told me."

"Well Jesse told you wrong, I never said that. Where is Jesse? Does he still live in Oaktown?"

"Where he's living ain't yo' business. Now you asking too many questions," Wanda retorted.

"Can you please just give me his number?" Yolanda begged.

"No, but I'll give him *your* number and if he wanna call you, he will," Wanda said and hung up before Yolanda could say another word.

Now Yolanda really felt like she was an extra in a horror movie. Had Jesse really tried to reach out to her? If so, when? Did Gwen really say that she didn't need Jesse to be a part of her life? The only way she would know the truth was to talk to Gwen.

Yolanda's stomach churned and her insides burned. She didn't want to believe it but her gut told her that what Wanda said was the truth. Just like Gwen didn't want Stanley in her life, she didn't want Jesse in her kids' lives, either.

CHAPTER 15

The message from Valerie on Stanley's phone made his day. She'd said that Sabrina was overjoyed about meeting him and had told everyone in their family that she and Stanley were on the way to a great relationship.

Valerie then invited him to an event at Sabrina's college. Some kind of "University Night," she'd said on the message. "I think Sabrina would be so excited and surprised to see you there. Give me a call."

Stanley had returned the call as soon as he'd clocked out and was in his vehicle. Though he was freezing, waiting for the heat to kick in, his heart was warm. "Hi, Valerie. I got your message. What's the event?"

"Oh, it's an event where the students who are entering their final semester at the junior college can meet with representatives of prospective schools, discuss credit transfers, and explore options for completing four-year degrees."

Stanley's chest filled with pride. "Oh, wow…that's cool."

"I'm sorry for the last-minute invitation. I was just thinking it might be something you'd want to do with us this evening."

Stanley envisioned himself standing next to Sabrina, looking over her shoulder protectively, listening as she asked questions about the academic programs while Stanley asked questions about campus security. The college representatives wouldn't know that Stanley hadn't been in Sabrina's life up until now. They'd treat him like a father.

And fifteen years from now, when he and Sabrina talk about her college years to her child, Sabrina would mention how Stanley

94

had been there when she was picking a university. This was an excellent memory in the making.

Stanley had hurriedly agreed to attend. "I can't wait."

"Great," Valerie said.

"What's the address to the college?"

"Oh, I figured you could just come by the house. You can follow us from here," she said.

It was all the same to him, so he agreed.

Stanley had rushed home, showered, changed clothes, and briefly told his mother about his impromptu plans.

"Tell Sabrina I said hello. And see if you can't bring her back here to me," his mother said between breaths from her oxygen mask.

Watching his mother struggle for air gave Stanley pause. "Momma, do you need me to stay here with you?"

She waved him off. "Naw. I'm fine. Me and the Lord got this. You go see about my grandbaby."

"Yes, ma'am," Stanley agreed.

He thanked God all the way to Sabrina's house. This was perfect. The kind of thing he'd seen fathers doing on TV shows. The only thing that would have made it better would have been if Kim and Yolanda had come, too. Then they could really make some good memories together.

If only Yolanda would cooperate. But Stanley remembered Debbie's words. He needed to give Yolanda time to realize that he was serious about his apology about the past as well as his intentions for the future.

Stanley parked in the driveway of Sabrina and Valerie's home. He hopped out of his truck and nearly skipped to the front door. He was as giddy as a grade school child on a field trip.

When the door swung open, Stanley's eyes flew wide open as well. There stood Valerie in a short, red, silk nightie with white, poofy fur on top. Her long legs shined with what must have been oil, and she wore open-toed high heels to make the look complete.

"Uhhh...ummm..." Stanley stuttered, utterly amazed at the sight of Valerie's body. She had more cellulite and a few more pounds on her since back in the day, but she was still a beautiful woman.

Valerie smiled. She pushed his chin back in place. "Come on in, Stanley." She tugged his hand and drew him inside the house. She shut the door behind him.

Stanley looked around. "Wh-where's Sabrina?"

"At school," Valerie nearly sang. "She has a late class tonight." Valerie put her arms around his waist and pulled him closer to her.

The room grew warm already.

"Stanley Brown, you don't know how long I've waited for this moment," Valerie said between kisses on his neck.

"Um, wait a second." Stanley stepped back an inch, which was as far as Valerie's grip would allow him to move. "Aren't we going to University Night?"

"That all depends," Valerie said. "I was thinking we could rock each other's worlds tonight. Isn't that kind of the same thing—the universe and the world?" She laughed seductively at her own joke.

Stanley's heart beat faster. From the waist up, he was thinking, *Wait a minute—I came here to help my daughter pick a university*. But from the waist down, the conversation was, *Yes! Finally! Forget Jesus – I got needs!* Stanley struggled to decide which part of his body to listen to.

"V-Valerie, I—"

"Don't speak, Stanley. Just act." She used the height of her heels to plant kisses on his neck. "We can pick up where we left off. You can move in. Find a job here," Valerie sputtered between kisses.

Stanley wasn't one for soap operas, but he had watched a few scenes here and there over the years and marveled at how dramatic some of the love scenes were. Right about now, Valerie was acting like an Emmy award-wining daytime actress.

"But, Valerie—"

"No, no, no," Valerie interrupted again. "I've never stopped loving you, and I'm sure you feel the same, otherwise you never would have come looking for me."

Love? He didn't love Valerie twenty-something years ago and he sure didn't love her now. "Wait a minute."

"I can't!" She wrapped her hand behind his head and pulled his lips into hers.

Her moist lips. Her crazy words. Stanley couldn't breathe. He couldn't think.

Until he heard, "Mother! Dad! What are you doing?!" from behind.

A loud smack occurred as their lips separated. Stanley turned to see Sabrina's shocked face.

"What is going on? Is *this* why you came back into my life? To get with my mother?" Sabrina screamed.

The sadness in her eyes was almost unbearable for Stanley. "No, sweetheart, I—"

"Don't *sweetheart* me!" Sabrina threw her purse on the couch.

"Sabrina, don't be so dramatic." Valerie shushed her.

Stanley looked at Valerie like she was out of her mind.

Valerie continued, "Your father and I were once very much in love, and you know what they say—old flames never die. We're rekindling the flame." She grabbed a throw blanket from the love seat and covered herself.

"No, we're not," Stanley finally objected. He didn't want to disrespect Valerie, but he couldn't have Sabrina thinking that his efforts to reunite as father and daughter hadn't been genuine. "I came here to help you choose a college."

"I'm already *in* college."

"No! Your next college," Stanley tried to explain. He turned to Valerie for help. "University night, right?" He made a sweeping motion for Valerie to intervene.

Sabrina crossed her arms. "University night isn't until next month."

Valerie shrugged. "My bad."

Stanley exhaled and tried to start at the beginning. "Your mother called me today and—"

"And you came right over and we were just about to get things started until you came home."

Sabrina's eyes filled with tears. "I can't believe you. Stanley." She stomped off down the hallway. Stanley attempted to follow her, but Valerie grabbed his arm and twirled him around to face her.

She whispered, "Stanley, she's a kid. She'll get over it. You and I are the parents here and we owe it to each other to try again."

Valerie ripped off the blanket and threw it to the ground. "Stanley, let's start over again. We would make great parents for Sabrina. She's a good kid—we're good together, obviously."

For the first time that evening, Stanley actually processed the words coming out of Valerie's mouth.

She must have caught wind of his contemplation. She pressed into him. "Neither of us is getting any younger. What do we have to lose? Move here. We can work out the details later. Sabrina will understand."

Stanley breathed deeply. It was freezing outside these days and the dock was rough on a brother's aging bones. And he had to admit to himself that the idea of standing next to Sabrina as she moved forward in life wasn't a bad picture. So what if Valerie was there, too? She wasn't a bad person. Desperate, but not mean like Rhonda and Gwen, and she probably wouldn't demand as much of him as a woman like Debbie would.

But there was another consideration—his growth in Christ.

"Could you please put that blanket back on? I can't think straight with you standing here like…this," Stanley admitted.

Valerie laughed but honored his request.

He sat down on the love seat, across from her.

"What do you say?" Valerie reiterated.

"I'm not the same man I used to be," Stanley stated to her as much as himself. Turning down a half-naked woman was a first for him. An absolute first.

"I see," she agreed. "The Stanley Brown I remember was always good for a roll in the hay without a moment's notice. But I guess age catches up to us all."

"It's not about my age."

"Well alrighty then." She purred.

"No. I mean…I'm changed on the *inside*. Different priorities. Different ideas about life. I'm going to church now. Even thinking about becoming a deacon."

"A *what?*" Valerie busted out laughing

"Yes. A deacon," Stanley repeated with a straight face.

"Well, if you can be a deacon, I can be a first lady one of these days," she joked. "I ain't no heathen, you know. I got my religion real young."

Stanley questioned, "So…you have a relationship with Christ?" Maybe if Valerie was a struggling new believer like him, they could help each other out.

She pulled the blanket tightly around her. "I sure do. I put God first in *everything* I do."

Stanley nodded. "That's good about God and all. I'm asking you about Jesus, though. I mean…do you know *Him*, too?"

"God, Jesus, the Universe, Allah, Karma—it's all the same," she spat with a wave of her hand.

That was all Stanley needed to hear. He stood, fighting the waist-down voice screaming in his mind. "Valerie, I'm sorry. As beautiful as you are and as tempting as this whole situation is, we're not on the same page. I don't want to hurt you and I certainly don't want to hurt Sabrina."

She cocked her head to the side. "So that's it?"

"I'd like to remain cordial, for our daughter's sake," Stanley said.

"Some things haven't changed, Stanley. Here I am again playing the fool for you."

"I'm sorry about that last time, Valerie, but you deserve better than how I treated you then. You're a beautiful, smart woman. You've raised a wonderful daughter. You have a lot to offer the right man for you."

Her face became suddenly somber. "But that man's not you, huh?"

"No, I'm afraid not." Stanley looked down the hallway. "You really think Sabrina will be okay?"

"Yeah. Give her a day or two."

"Will you tell her the truth?" Stanley asked.

"Don't worry about what I do. Just call her and keep being your same old charming self. She may fall for it the same as I always did."

Stanley wanted to dash down the hall and find Sabrina to let her know how sorry he was that this whole thing looked so shady. But he knew from experience that sometimes he just needed to let a woman cool off before he said anything else. Otherwise, they'd twist every word he said in so many knots, he would be confused by the end of the conversation.

"Good night, Valerie."

"Mmm hmm."

Stanley let himself out and got into his truck. *Lord, I've come too far to lose Sabrina now. Comfort her heart and let her listen to me when the time is right. In Jesus' name, Amen.*

CHAPTER 16

K im stepped out of the long, black, stretch limousine that
Larry had rented for the evening. The dress she wore was
a beautiful black gown made of soft, satiny fabric, long
and loose. Kim waited for the attendant to open the door before
she got out. The photographer she hired took pictures of her like
he was the paparazzi.

When Kim opened the door to the ballroom she felt like she
was in a fairy tale. The dining room was elegant. Each table had
silver tablecloths covered with red rose petals and an array of red
and pink roses for the centerpiece.

"Ladies and gentlemen, please help me welcome my beautiful
daughter, Ms. Kimberley Ann Maxwell," Larry said on the DJ's
microphone.

Kim walked down the long, red carpet that was also covered in
rose petals waving like she was Miss America. She took her honored seat at the main table.

All of her friends and co-workers applauded; Larry made his
way up to the microphone. "Thanks so much for being here with
me tonight, to help me celebrate my beautiful daughter. Tonight,
we are going to party like it's 1999!"

Kim hid her face in her hands as she laughed.

"DJ, take it away!" her father hollered.

When her father came to the table, Kim kissed him and whispered into his ear, "Dad, no one says we're gonna party like it's
1999 anymore."

"What?" He was shocked. "When did we stop sayin' that?"

"Ummm…in 1999."

Larry laughed so hard Kim could see the tears forming. She kissed him again on his cheek. "But I love you anyway, Dad."

"Love you, too, Kim."

She left him for the dance floor. Kim's cousin Wayne joined her on the dance floor and started a line dance. Sherry and Larry followed suit.

After a few more dances, Kim headed to her table to take a break.

She pulled out her cell phone to call Yolanda.

The phone went straight to voicemail.

She probably ain't coming.

"Baaaaaby this party is fire! You need to hook me up with one of your old classmates," her cousin Brandy said.

"Brandy, I am not a matchmaker. The last time I tried to hook you up, it didn't work."

"It ain't my fault. He wanted too much too soon."

"How is wanting to get married after a year of dating too much too soon?"

"Kim, I don't want a husband. I just want someone to hang out with, you know, kick it with."

"Kicking it days are over with, Brandy. I don't know about you but I want a husband."

"I heard when you get older you start talking crazy. You just confirmed it." Brandy laughed.

"You're only a year younger than me, and besides what's wrong with wanting to be a wife?"

"Ummm ain't nothing wrong with wanting to be a wife, especially if he looks like ole dude over there. I said the next man I get would be older anyway. Hook me up with him." Brandy pointed to the door.

"Girl, that's my father."

"Well I might be double kin to you then! Dang, he fine."

"Brandy, that's my father for real. That's my biological father, Stanley Brown."

"Oh snap. I thought you was playing, but dang he still fine, though."

"Kim, is that who I think it is?" Sherry rushed over to the table and asked.

"Yes, Mom, that's Stanley. I'm going to get him so he'll know where I'm sitting."

"Why didn't you warn that he was coming?" Sherry said breathing heavily.

"Mom, it's my birthday. I wanted him here. Please, just be nice."

"Aunt Sherry, he fine. Can't believe you let him get away."

Both Kim and Sherry gave Brandy a scolding look.

"I'm just saying. The Bible says tell the truth 'cause it will set you free. Just trying to be obedient." Brandy grinned.

"Kim, you go ahead and take a seat at the head so we can get started with the formals. I'll go say hello to your father," Sherry instructed.

Kim gripped her mother's arm. "Mom. Remember. Be nice."

Sherry sighed. The line in her forehead smoothed out. "I will. Tonight is about you. I just want Stanley Brown to know that he needs to be on his best behavior."

"That goes for everybody here," Kim said by way of warning.

"I hear you."

"Pinky swear?" She held up her pinky finger.

Sherry laughed, returning the gesture. "Pinky swear."

The look on Sherry's face hadn't been as welcoming as Stanley had been hoping for.

"Look what the cat drug in," she said under her breath as Stanley took two hors d'oeuvres from an attendant.

Her remark caught Stanley off guard. "It's like that?"

Sherry curled her index finger toward her face. Stanley followed her to a side corner nearest the entrance of the large room.

When she got him to herself and out of the view of most of the guests, she whispered, "Lucky for you, Kim has a heart of gold. All I know is, you'd better not break it or you'll have me *and* my husband to answer to."

Before Stanley could defend his intentions, he found himself face-to-face with a man just as tall and broad as himself.

"Stanley?"

"Yes. Stanley Brown."

The man stuck out a hand. "Larry Maxwell. I'm Kim's Dad."

Stanley pumped Larry's hand firmly and looked him dead in the eyes. "It's my pleasure to finally meet you and shake your hand, Larry. I can't thank you enough for the wonderful job you and Sherry have done with Kim."

Sherry's eyebrow shot up as though she couldn't believe what she'd heard. "Excuse me?"

"Looks to me like you two have given her the best of everything. More than I could have ever done...better than I could have done. I owe you more than I could ever repay."

Larry looked down at Sherry. Her eyes misted slightly.

"Watching Kim go from a little girl with pigtails and glasses into a young woman has been one of my life's greatest pleasures," Larry said. "I have no regrets."

"I wish I could say the same," Stanley admitted. "I've missed out on a lot. And I know you'll always be the first man in her life. You two are the most important people, the ones she has come to know and depend on. I know I haven't done much...well, I've done nothing until now. I just...all I want to do is add to the number of people rooting for her."

Larry gazed into Sherry's eyes. Sherry's demeanor softened.

Larry nodded at Stanley. "Welcome to team Kim." He slapped Stanley on the back and the three of them entered the festivities at hand.

Stanley sat between two of Kim's uncles and watched in awe as person after person told of how Kim had helped them through so many of life's events through encouragement, prayer, and even financially.

When Kim finally took the microphone, after a dinner consisting of grilled pork chops, salad, sweet potatoes, and green beans, Stanley joined the dinner guests as they clapped when Kim honored her parents. Next, she thanked two close friends, her pastor, and family members who had obviously played major parts in their lives. When Kim thanked a male friend for coming, Stanley's protective instincts kicked in. *Who is that joker?* He'd have to ask Kim about that guy later.

"Finally, I'd like to thank the newest edition to my life," Kim said as her green eyes settled on Stanley's. "I've shared with some of you that I've recently reconnected with my biological father, Stanley Brown." She motioned toward him and the audience clapped. "He hasn't been a part of my past, but I do look forward to him being a part of my future. Thanks for coming."

Stanley's heart swelled with all the love and pride he could stand. And the smile that plastered his face as he took selfies with Kim never left his face. He changed his screensaver to a picture of Kim with Larry, Sherry, and himself later that night.

CHAPTER 17

Yolanda heard her phone buzzing but decided not to answer when she saw the call was from Kim. Tonight was the night of Kim's birthday party and she didn't want to explain to her why she wasn't coming. She at first thought about going but then realized that she didn't have anything to wear.

This would have been a great night to get out, especially since the kids were at a church lock in with her neighbor's kids. But the main reason Yolanda didn't want to go was because she didn't want to run into Stanley. She was certain that Kim had invited him, with his trifling self. Yolanda still didn't understand how Kim could be so forgiving and how Grandma Effie basically gave him a "you don't have to be a father" pass just because his father had abandoned him. Yolanda wasn't about to let Deontae and Eric off the hook with her future grandkids.

The phone buzzed again and this time it was to notify her that she had notifications from Facebook.

All of the notifications were from Kim. She'd posted 50 pictures and a video from the party. Yolanda clicked through the pictures and saw a picture of Kim with Stanley. He was dressed nice; he wore a black two-button tuxedo with a white shirt and a black bow tie. Stanley had his arm around her and they both smiled as if they were in a toothpaste commercial, showing all of their teeth.

Yolanda stared at the picture a little while longer. She had to admit to herself that a part of her wished that she would have been there. The pictures and video confirmed that they had a great time. On the video Kim and Larry were dancing to "Dance With My

Father" by Luther Vandross and in the middle of the song Larry motioned for Stanley to come and finish the dance.

Yolanda couldn't contain herself. She began to cry and her tears flowed profusely. The pain of not having her father hit her like a ton of bricks. She clutched her pillow. She needed something to hold unto. The sobs were stifled at first, but the wave of emotions turned her cry into a moan.

"What in the world is going on?" Gwen stormed into Yolanda's room.

Yolanda tried to find the words to talk but her sobs wouldn't stop.

"Answer me," Gwen demanded.

"It's nothing," Yolanda said, trying to gather herself.

"It has to be something. You in here crying like somebody done died. Now tell me the truth."

"I just saw a video of Kim dancing with Stanley and—"

"And that made you cry?" Gwen said, cutting her off.

"Yes, it made me cry," she fessed up. "I know you don't like Stanley and I know you think he's up to no good, but I really hate that I didn't have him in my life."

"That was a decision *he* made," Gwen pointed out.

"That might have been the decision he made back then, but what if he really is a changed man now? I could be missing an opportunity to be in his life just because you said so."

Gwen took a deep breath and sat on the bed. "So you think just because he showed up out the blue and does a dance with Kim, he's a changed man? Stanley Brown is up to something. Trust me. I know."

"How do you know? You haven't seen him in years."

"'Cause if it walk like a duck, talk like a duck, it's a duck, that's how I know," Gwen yelled. "I'm trying to keep you from getting hurt."

"Were you trying to keep me from getting hurt by telling Jesse

CaSandra McLaughlin & Michelle Stimpson

you had no idea where I was?" Yolanda spat and stood face to face with Gwen.

"Who told you that?"

"Just answer the question?" Yolanda ordered.

"Now look a here, I know you call yourself mad but I'm still your mother, so watch your tone." Gwen pointed her finger at Yolanda. "Yes, I told Jesse not to call me anymore looking for you. That boy ain't nothing but a screw up, and I don't want him around my grandchildren."

"Mama, you don't get to decide who can and can't be in my life. That's *my* choice."

"Can't you see that Jesse is just like Stanley?" Gwen threw her hands up in the air.

"Deontae, Eric, and Zoey need their father just like I need mine. I refuse to allow you to keep their father from them the way you are trying to keep mine away from me."

"Yolanda. Stanley left me. I was good to that man and he left me with nothing, and now you want to welcome him with open arms," Gwen shouted. "How dare you turn your back on me. I took care of you. I struggled to make sure you had somewhat of a good life." Gwen fought back her tears.

"I am not turning my back on you. I just need to see where things could go with Stanley. I don't know what it's like to have a father, and now I have another chance. I'm not going to turn my back on taking a chance because you are still bitter behind your break up."

"Who said I was bitter? Oh, so now you're my counselor?" Gwen rolled her eyes.

"I didn't say I was a counselor but it's obvious that you haven't forgiven him because if you had, you wouldn't be so upset," Yolanda snapped.

"Yolanda, look, you don't know what all I went through with Stanley. I loved that man. He was my whole world. He made me

108

so many promises and he broke every last one of them. Can you imagine how I felt when he left with no explanation?"

"Yes I can imagine because that's how I felt when Jesse and I broke up. I had to get over him, but I can't punish him by not letting him be a part of our children's lives. I don't want them to grow up saying that I kept them from their dad. They deserve to know their father and if he screws things up that's on him but at least I did my part." She took a deep breath and asked, "Did you ever wonder about your dad?"

The question caught Gwen off guard. Talking about her dad was something she never did. "I thought about my father a lot, but I knew not to mention him to my mother. I remember asking her to call him to come to my championship volleyball game, but she wouldn't. All of my teammate's parents were there. I wanted my father there, too." The tears that Gwen tried to hold onto came streaming down her face.

"I… I… always wanted to know if he even cared about me," she wailed.

"Oh, Mom. I'm sorry." Yolanda hugged her. "Did you ever hear from him?"

"No I didn't hear from him. I don't even know who he is." Gwen lowered her head and covered her face in embarrassment.

Yolanda pulled Gwen into her arms and rocked her for a while in silence.

This shared moment between the two had never happened. Gwen had never allowed herself to be vulnerable until now.

"Mom, I don't want my children to end up like us. I have to do what's best for them," Yolanda said.

"I guess you're right. If that's what you want for your kids, I can't stop you, and I can't stop you from being in Stanley's life either. Just please don't tell Stanley where I live. I don't ever want to see him again." Gwen retrieved a Kleenex off the nightstand and blew her nose.

"I can respect your wishes," Yolanda agreed.

"I wish I knew how to contact Jesse. Deontae has been asking about him. I can't keep lying to him."

"I might be able to help you solve that problem. Just a minute." Gwen left the room and returned with a small piece of paper. "This is the number that came up on the caller ID the last time he called. Now, that was a while ago but hopefully you'll be able to contact him. I was wrong for keeping this from you. I thought I was helping you but it seems like I did more harm than good. Please forgive me, Yolanda."

"I forgive you, Mama. I love you."

"I love you, too, baby. I just don't want to see you hurt. Guess I have to realize you're not a little girl anymore. I have to let you grow up and make your own decisions."

"Thanks, Mama." They hugged.

Gwen left Yolanda's room and closed the door behind her.

Yolanda's hands were sweating as she slowly dialed Jesse's number. Her heart skipped a few beats when he answered.

"Hello."

"Jesse, hey this is Yolanda," she said calmly.

There was a brief moment of silence.

"Jesse, are you there?"

"Yeah, I'm here. How did you get my number?" He stuttered.

"My mom gave it to me." She held her breath and waited for his reply.

"I have been trying to reach you."

"I know. Wanda told me."

"Yolanda if you are calling about the child support, I just started back working a month ago so I am sure you'll get something soon. How are my kids doing?" he asked.

"They're fine. Deontae has been asking about you. That's what I was calling you about. I want you to be in their lives."

"I want the same thing, and that's why I was calling your mom's house. You changed your cell phone and cut me off."

"I was upset about us, but this isn't about us. This is about the kids."

"Yolanda, I'm sorry for putting you through so much. I won't say it was because I was young. I was just plain selfish," Jesse admitted.

"I accept your apology and I hope that we can at least be friends for the kids' sake," she offered.

"Cool, that's what's up. I want to see my kids. Are you living with your mom?"

"Yes, I am still living with my mom." She perked up. The conversation with Jesse was going better than she expected.

"I live in Merdis, but I can come there."

"Merdis? What made you move out there?" Merdis was an hour away from Jaxton and there was nothing in the small town. They only had a gas station, grocery store, Wal-Mart, and Dairy Queen.

"My job is out here, so I had no choice. The drive back and forward would have been too much on my car. I'm off on weekends, so can I come by and see the kids tomorrow?"

"Let's meet up somewhere. I'll text you the details tomorrow."

"Alright, talk to you tomorrow, Yo-Yo," Jesse said, using her nickname he'd given her when they were dating.

"Okay. Bye, Jesse." Yolanda hung up the phone feeling hopeful. She couldn't wait for the kids to see Jesse.

CHAPTER 18

S tanley placed the bookmark with this month's memory verses at his stopping point in Psalm 91. He, along with the rest of the brethren of Warren Grove, had committed to memorizing this chapter for the month of February. Though it was only the first Sunday of the month, Stanley had memorized the first seven verses already. He was both amazed and encouraged at how often the words came to him throughout the day, reminding him of God's protection and love. It was as though God Himself was whispering to Stanley at the most opportune times. *Thank You, Father*, was all Stanley had time to whisper back as he busied himself on the forklift.

This morning, as Stanley was getting ready for church, he repeated the verses he'd memorized three times. Then he went to the kitchen and prepared breakfast for his mother.

She was already up in the living room watching televangelists. His mother might not have been a big church-goer, and she'd kicked up her fair share of dust back in the day, but she was serious about revering God on Sundays. No washing clothes or cars, no yard work, no heavy cooking, no cussing, drinking, or smoking on the Sabbath.

He couldn't count the number of times he'd heard his mother say, "I don't play with God," when it came to some of the religious things she held sacred. Stanley wished his mother had a day-to-day relationship with God because, as he was discovering, it sure was helpful to keep Him and His ways first and foremost seven days a week.

"Made you that chicken sausage you like," Stanley said as he set her plate on the TV tray. "You need anything else?"

Effie thanked him. "This is fine. And you sure look mighty fine, too. Nice and acceptable."

Stanley wasn't sure how to take her words. Rather than speculate, he asked, "What do you mean by that?"

"I mean you sure look like one of them mens of God. The kind that be readin' scriptures and prayin' over the congregation. Like a deacon."

He straightened his tie. "I told you, that *is* my goal."

"Well, looks can be deceiving. You talked to *all* your daughters yet?"

The way his mother could switch gears without notice was truly a talent all her own. "Yes, I have. Things are going very well with Kim."

"What about Yolanda and Sabrina?"

He poked out his lips for a moment, trying to figure out how to explain things. "Yolanda's still angry. Sabrina was doing well, but then she fell under the impression that I was trying to get back with Valerie and some confusion has come up. I have to clear up the misconception as soon as possible—but that will all depend on if and when she returns my calls and text messages."

Effie chewed a bit of her sausage. "Well, you gotta be persistent, Stanley. I know that ain't one of your strong points up until now. But I see you changin', son. God's gonna reward you for it. You done messed over a bunch of people for a long time. The ideas they been havin' in their minds about you all this time won't change overnight. You got to keep at it over time in order to convince people."

"Yes, ma'am," Stanley agreed, thinking that he sure could have used this speech twenty years ago. "Momma, why are you telling me all of this now?"

Her fork clanked as she laid it on the glass plate. "Well, I ain't delusional. I know my time is winding up. I don't want to leave my family in a mess. I know I ain't no church-goin' woman, but I do love the Lord and I do pray, and He is answering my prayers about you and all my family, starting with your sister. She been carin' for everybody else all her life. She got such a giving heart, but the doctors told her a long time ago she couldn't have no babies. She thought that meant she would never be of use to anybody except me. So I prayed for her to get a good husband who'll take care of her and wasn't lookin' to have no kids. Sure enough, that's exactly what happened. And I prayed for you, too, to get your life right. And now here you are. Standing before me in your Sunday best, on your way to church. God answers my prayers, all right."

Stanley smiled to himself. Maybe he had been wrong about his mother's relationship with God. "Thank you, Momma."

"Mighty welcome. Now, look at that pad and paper I got over there and get Yolanda's number. You got to call her, send her them readin' messages on her phone, go on Spacebook or whatever you got to do to chase her down so she'll know you serious. And say whatever you need to say to get back in Sabrina's good graces. You always had a way with women—use your powers for good this time, son."

"Yes, ma'am," he agreed with a chuckle.

Stanley found Yolanda's number and sent her a text as he got into his truck. *Yolanda, please call me. Just want to talk. —Stanley.*

The seniors' choir sang some old tunes Stanley had only heard at people's funerals. Almost put him to sleep. He was so glad when Pastor stood to deliver the sermon, which gave him a second wind of energy.

Pastor was preaching on Psalm 91 all month long, and now that Stanley was memorizing the chapter, the sermon made even more sense.

Stanley thought of how Kim's relationship with God had started so young, according to her testimony at the birthday party last night. She had known Him for most of her life. Stanley was almost jealous of how much better her life was going because she had come to Christ at an early age. The assurance, the love, the peace—no wonder she had so easily received Stanley back into her life again. Her relationship with God made it easier to relate to people.

Right then and there, with that understanding, Stanley made up his mind that he would begin to pray for both Yolanda and Sabrina to come into the knowledge of God, too—and the sooner the better. Not just so that they would be closer to Stanley, but so they could experience life with the Word of God guiding their every step. If God has listened to Effie's prayers, he would probably listen to Stanley's, too.

Following the altar call, there were a few church announcements. Then Deacon Lewis took the side podium. "Saints and friends, haven't we had a wonderful time in the Lord?"

"Amen," the congregants agreed in unison.

"I know you all are getting hungry, so I won't be before you long."

The crowd laughed.

"I just wanted to let you all know that the Deacon's board is planning to grow by a few more in the coming weeks. And we wanted to let you all know that there are several men in our midst who have volunteered to help our church by donating their time and talents, serving Warren Grove Church unselfishly as Deacons. We haven't made our final selections yet, but we believe they all deserve a hand. It takes a lot to subject yourself to the scrutiny of fellow church members. So even if they are not selected as deacons, any of them would make fine auxiliary leaders."

Stanley's stomach knotted up.

"I'd like for our prospective deacons to stand."

Stanley waited for someone else to take the lead. Once he saw one head rising, he quickly stood as well, so as not to appear shy.

The congregation clapped and cheered. Stanley and four other men stood humbly. The applause, as good as it was, didn't quite mean as much to Stanley as he had thought it would. All these people in the room celebrating him was, at this point, just the gravy on top of what God had done in his heart and with his children.

"Would any of you like to have words before we make our final selections?" Deacon Lewis asked. "I know I'm putting you all on the spot. But that's part of being a Deacon—representing the church at a moment's notice."

Stanley raised his hand slightly. When Deacon Lewis removed the microphone from its holder, Stanley declined. "I think I can speak loudly enough."

"Go ahead, Brother."

Stanley felt the words flowing up from his heart. "I just want to thank the church for giving me this opportunity to offer my service to the body of Christ. I've got a lot of catching up to do." They laughed at his joke. "The truth is, whether I actually become a Deacon this time around or not doesn't matter. The process of proving myself an upstanding man before you all has actually changed me into one. And for that alone, I am grateful."

Nods and approving smiles emanated from the audience.

"Like he said," Stanley continued, "I'm willing to serve in another capacity. No problem. Just don't put me on the hospitality committee 'cause I can't cook."

The audience roared in laughter and Stanley took his seat.

This had been good for him. Real good. *Thank You, Lord.*

Later that night, Stanley got the call from Deacon Lewis that he had indeed been approved as a Deacon. This was the icing on top of the cake.

CHAPTER 19

S abrina sat in the middle of her bed scrolling through her re-
corded TV shows. She was glad to have some down time.
She had spent most of her time at the school library just so
that she could hide from Valerie. She had avoided her as much as
she possibly could. With Valerie constantly showing houses and
schmoozing with city officials at galas and other networking events,
it was easy to dodge her mother. Sabrina didn't want to have to talk
to her about what happened with Stanley. Sabrina refused to call or
text him. She was done with Stanley.

"Sabrina. Sabrina I know you hear me calling you," Valerie
yelled from the living room.

Sabrina didn't move. She quickly turned the TV off, rolled over
on her side, got under the covers, and pretended to be asleep.

Valerie entered the room and walked over to Sabrina's bed. "I
know you're not asleep." Valerie snatched the cover off her daughter.

Sabrina still didn't move and kept her eyes closed.

"I don't have time to play games with you. Enough is enough.
I refuse to let another day go by without talking to you." Sabrina
still made no movement. "Sabrina please answer me."

Sabrina stayed in place.

"Pleeeeeease," she said, shaking Sabrina.

"Mom, I really don't have anything to say," Sabrina finally answered.

"Look, if we're going to stop talking to one another, it might
as well be over something true, not a lie. So here goes the truth: It

was my fault, Sabrina. Stanley really is innocent."

"Yea right," Sabrina said, sitting up.

"Honestly, it was all me. I invited him here under false pretenses. I wanted him to come back to me," Valerie confessed.

"Why are you trying to cover for him?" Sabrina asked slightly irritated.

"Sabrina, how would Stanley know about your college night? You never told him. I set the whole thing up. I was so focused on getting him back that I didn't think about how that would make you feel." Valerie sat beside her.

It never dawned on Sabrina that she never told Stanley about college night. The only thing she was focused on was the fact that she caught him kissing Valerie.

"How could you do this to me?" Sabrina pouted.

"It's not about you. I've been loving Stanley for a long time. I was hoping that he would feel the same way, but unfortunately that wasn't the case. He's a changed man. Can you find it in your heart to forgive me?"

"I'll forgive you, if you promise me you'll give up on the idea of trying to get him back."

"I'm convinced that Stanley is either a changed man or he's playing for the other team now. I'm settling on the latter because I know it's hard to turn down all of this." Valerie stood up and strutted her stuff.

"Mom, stop it." Sabrina clasped her hands over her mouth.

"Well, I'm just saying." Valerie laughed. "But seriously, I think you should give your dad a call."

"Well…he did send me a text inviting me to his ordination ceremony. He's going to be a deacon."

"I think you should go. He'd be glad to see you there. I'll come with you if you want me to."

"Hmmmm, I think I'll be just fine." Sabrina side-eyed her mother.

"What?" Valerie giggled. "I'll be on my best behavior, I promise."

"Thanks for the offer, but I think this is something I need to do on my own."

"Okie dokie, kiddo."

"Mom, thanks for clearing things up."

"You're welcome." Valerie kissed her on the cheek and left the room.

Sabrina was glad that she'd been wrong about Stanley. She was looking forward to having him in her life and spending quality time with him and possibly her sisters.

She searched her purse and grabbed her phone to text him.

Hey Dad, got your message, I'd love to come to the ordination.

He replied: *You just made my day! And thanks for responding, looking forward to seeing you again.*

Sabrina replied: *Me too!*

Two weeks had passed since Kim's birthday party and today she was meeting Yolanda for lunch. They hadn't really talked since seeing Grandma Effie at the hospital.

Kim pulled into Gurtie's Catfish and made her way inside.

Gurtie's was a small, dainty, family owned establishment. The decor was simple. Each table had a red, white, and black checkered tablecloth. The standard salt, pepper, ketchup, and hot sauce sat on every table. The owner, Gurtie Burns, was known for her homemade coleslaw and tartar sauce. Gurtie's was the hot spot for catfish in Jaxton.

Kim settled in a booth and scanned the menu while she waited on Yolanda.

"Hello, I'm Calvin, and I'll be your waiter today," a tall, slender, caramel brother said. "May I take your drink order?"

"Yes, I'd like Gurtie's Classic Punch. I hope it's as good as it sounds."

"It's my favorite. It's a mixture of kool aids with flavored tea. You'll love it." He flashed his million dollar smile.

"Are you waiting on someone, or are you ready to order now?"

"My sister is actually pulling up now, so give us a few minutes," Kim said, looking out of the window.

"I'll get your drink and check back in a few minutes."

"Sounds good."

Kim waved to Yolanda as she walked in.

"Hey, sis." Kim stood up and gave her a hug.

"Hey. Sorry I'm late."

"Oh, no problem. I've only been here for a few minutes. Glad you're here."

"Yea, me, too." Yolanda took her jacket off and placed it beside her.

"Are you ladies ready to order?" Calvin asked and placed Kim's drink in front of her.

"So what's the best thing to order?" Kim asked.

"I'm getting the catfish and shrimp special. It's really good," Yolanda said.

"Okay, I'll have the same." Kim took a swig of her drink. "Oooh, this is too good."

"Bring me whatever she's drinking," Yolanda added.

"Alright that's two catfish and shrimp specials and another Classic punch. I'll put those orders in and be back with your drink in a few minutes."

Calvin left and both Yolanda and Kim sat there for a minute, each waiting on the other to start the conversation. Yolanda finally broke the ice.

"Kim, I'm sorry for what I said to you at the hospital. I didn't really mean it. I was just upset."

"I accept your apology, that's water under the bridge. I will say

I was a little hurt that you didn't come to my birthday party."

"I didn't want to see Stanley. I'm not really sure that I can welcome him with open arms the way that you have."

"I can understand how you feel. I really am glad that I'm getting to know him. Did you know we have a sister and a brother?"

"I've heard about Sabrina, but where did our brother come from? Are you sure?" Yolanda asked.

"Our brother, Todderick, was killed and our sister, Sabrina, lives in Wayville. They were born just a few months apart. Must have been a whole bunch of drama, I'm sure." Kim shook her head. "That's all I know for now."

"You think he's hiding something?" Yolanda speculated.

"No," Kim said. "I mean, he hasn't skirted around the fact that he was a terrible person and a terrible father. There's nothing else to lie about. I'm sure there's more to the details to his story, but the worst is out. It's going to take a while to sort through all these missing years."

"Grandma Effie told me about Sabrina, but she's never mentioned Todderick. This is just crazy. Stanley was spreading his love in every city. Maybe we should go on The Steve Harvey Show and have him to locate all our siblings. I bet you it's enough of us to start a football team." Yolanda laughed.

Calvin brought out the orders and Yolanda's drink and placed them on the table. "Ladies enjoy your meal, and please let me know if you need anything else."

"Okay, we will." Kim batted her eyes at him. "He's a little cutie, isn't he?"

"Kim, he's working at a fish joint, so I know he's not your type," Yolanda said, pouring ketchup on her fries.

"Now why would you say that?"

"Let's be real."

"Oh yeah, you right. This shrimp is delicious." Kim smacked her lips.

"Anyway, finish telling me about Todderick and Sabrina. What happened to Todderick?"

"Stanley said he was hanging out with the wrong crowd. He didn't get to attend the funeral. Todderick's mother sent him an obituary in the mail."

"Girl, naw! That's a mess. She must really be upset with Stanley."

"I guess so, but that's still wrong. She could have at least called Grandma Effie and told her about the funeral."

"So what's the deal with Sabrina?" Yolanda took a sip of her punch.

"She lives with her mother. She's a college student, in her twenties. Hopefully we'll get to meet her at the ordination. Are you coming?" Kim asked.

"I'm not sure."

"Well at least you didn't say no, so I'm going to pray that you and the kids will come. How are the kids?"

"They're doing good. They are with Jesse this weekend." Yolanda smiled.

"What? With who? Did you say *Jesse*?" Kim asked between chews.

"Yes, you heard me right. They are with Jesse. We've been communicating and he's stepping up to help out."

"Yolanda, that's great. I'm so happy for you and for them. They need their father. You need yours, too, so please think about giving things a try with Stanley. You have nothing to lose, and I really believe that he's ready to be there for us."

"How can you be so sure?"

"Both times I have been around him, he seems to be real sincere. He honestly just wants to get to know us."

"But why *now*?" Yolanda asked.

"As people grow in Christ they change. I believe God is working on him, and that's why he wants to make things right. It's never too late to get things right," Kim said with pleading eyes.

"Don't look at me like that. I said I would think about."

"That's all I'm asking."

The deliciousness of the meal tore them away from conversation for a while. Both ladies remarked on how tender and yet crispy the fish was and the tasty sides. Kim even broke the etiquette rules and licked her fingertips.

"Watch out now," Yolanda teased. "Got some 'hood coming out of you."

They laughed at the joke.

Calvin approached as they were laughing. "Did you ladies enjoy the meal? Would you like some dessert?"

"No, I'm too full," Kim said.

"Yeah me, too. Just give us the ticket," Yolanda said.

"I have it right here, and I forgot to ask if you guys were together or separate so I put it all on one ticket."

"That's okay. Here, just put it on my card." Kim gave him her credit card.

"Alright, I'll be right back."

"I could have paid for my meal," Yolanda stated.

"It's okay, sis. You can treat the next time." Kim winked at her.

Calvin brought Kim her credit card back and she and Yolanda thanked him.

"I enjoyed lunch. We should do this more often and hopefully the next time Sabrina will be with us," Kim said.

"Yea, hopefully so." Yolanda smiled as they both stood to leave.

"Alrighty, chic. Love you."

"Love you too, Kim."

The two sisters hugged and parted ways with hopes of seeing each other again soon. Kim was hoping that "soon" would be the next day.

CHAPTER 20

His tie was straight. Head shaved. Lips protected with Chapstick, though there was little chance they might be crusty because spring seemed to have arrived early that third Sunday in February.

Stanley stopped and looked at himself in the full-length mirror hanging on his closet door. Today was the day. His ordination. Not since graduating from High School had Stanley been honored or recognized in front of a crowd of people.

He wasn't sure of exactly who would come to the ordination. Debbie would be there, of course, because it was taking place right after the Sunday sermon. His mother was coming. Pastor Lee said he'd be there, too.

Kim would be there, certainly, and probably Sabrina per her text the previous night. But if Sabrina came, would Valerie come, too? He sure didn't want to see Valerie after that fiasco. He wanted today to be perfect.

But it couldn't be one hundred percent perfect without Yolanda.

Debbie had said that Yolanda needed more time, and Stanley was willing to give her all the time she needed to trust him.

Too bad it meant she would miss one of the most important days of his life.

He couldn't stand there staring at his handsome reflection worrying about Yolanda, though, because he sure didn't want to be late to church the day of his ordination. He smiled at himself, thinking, *So this is what it's like to be a real parent—worrying about your kids all the time.* Thankfully, he was learning the Scriptures like nobody's business. The assurances in the Word gave him the comfort and the security to avoid the feeling of helplessness he'd been dodging all his life. As he understood God's heart more, Stanley realized that one of the reasons he'd avoided being a father was because he didn't know what to do or how to be with such a weighty responsibility. If he knew then what he knew now, he would have realized that help was available to teach him what his own father didn't.

Still, all he could do was thank God for showing him when He did and move forward at this point.

Since his mother couldn't lift herself into the truck, Stanley had arranged for a special van to take her on to the church earlier.

Stanley rode to the church alone, thinking of what he'd say when the microphone was given to him. He had a speech in his mind, something like singers say when they accept a Grammy Award. First thank God, then his mother, then Pastor Lee for shepherding him as a new Christian. He'd thank Pastor Roundtree for teaching him now, and Deacon Lewis for believing in him. And then his daughters. He would have Kim and Sabrina stand up.

And finally, if Debbie was smiling at him, he'd thank Debbie for her encouragement. He wished he could give her a title—his girlfriend, special lady friend, or something more significant—to put everybody on notice. But the truth was, he could only classify his relationship with Debbie as brother and sister in Christ.

When he'd prayed to God about going further with Debbie, he hadn't gotten an answer. The silence, however, was an answer in itself. As he continued in Bible study and fellowship, Stanley realized that this was how things went with Christians. The first connection was in Christ. Anything over and above that was gravy.

The church parking lot was full and Sunday school probably hadn't even dismissed yet. Stanley had to park on the curb. The other men who were being ordained must have had large families because their people were definitely in attendance that day.

Thankfully, the usher led Stanley straight to the front row where a seat had been reserved for him. Throughout the service, Stanley wanted to turn around and see where his people were. He'd even stood during one of the children's choir songs and clapped just so he'd have occasion to glance across the congregation, but he had only spotted his mother and Debbie and, of course, Pastor Lee in the pulpit. So many others were standing and clapping, too, that Stanley couldn't get a good visual snapshot.

What if they're not here? What if Kim had been playing a cruel trick on him, making him think that she accepted him in her life when, in actuality, all she wanted was vengeance. What if Sabrina and Valerie were only playing along so they could gather information to send to the Attorney General? What if Yolanda's sentiments were shared by all three of his daughters? What if Rhonda wanted to shoot him because Todderick was dead?

Stanley shook off the horrible thoughts and prayed silently. *Lord, Help.*

That help came very quickly in the form of a sermon on John 3:16. Pastor Roundtree started by saying that most of us had memorized this verse as children. The congregation as a whole agreed, though Stanley could not. He hadn't grown up in the church like the rest of these people.

Pastor continued, "But I want you to hear me loud and clear today, like this is the first time you have ever seen this scripture before. The problem with some of us is that we've heard it too much. Let it go in one ear and out the other like it's common, like it's not a miracle, like it's not the best news ever told on the face of the earth."

The crowd murmured with expectancy.

"I just want to talk about the first six words in the Scripture, actually. For God so loved the world."

"Uh huh," Deacon Reed blurted out from a side pew. "Preach, preach-a!"

Several people giggled.

Pastor eyed Stanley and the honorees. "Now, y'all need to take some notes from Deacon Reed here. If you gonna be a Deacon, you gotta back up the man of God when he preaches. Amen?"

The congregation laughed.

Stanley looked at Deacon Reed, who quickly nodded back at Stanley. With that simple gesture, all was well between them.

"For God so loved the world," Pastor repeated. "Not the perfect people. Not the church. Not the Pharisees. The *world*. That means the *lost*, those who didn't know His goodness existed. Those who have been blinded by the hurts and pains of life. Those who are so burdened by the cares of this life and the evil god of this world, our adversary—satan. He doesn't want us to know this kind of love. The kind of love that will give up its rights in order to save someone else. Sacrificial love, unconditional love, the kind of love you write home about. The kind of love you don't deserve. This is the love the Father has for you."

With those few sentences, Stanley felt free to whisper a different prayer. *God, I don't deserve to be a Deacon. I don't deserve another chance to be a father to my daughters. Todderick didn't deserve to grow up without a father, and I certainly didn't deserve Your salvation, but You gave it to me anyway because You are good. Help me to rely on Your mercy alone. Thank You, God. And help me to serve this church and my loved ones in a way that causes them to see Your love in ways they never have before.*

As with so many other sermons, Stanley took what he needed at the moment and let it marinate in his heart. He wondered if, one day, he'd be able to digest a full thirty-minutes worth of preaching all at once because, right now, he was already full after only five minutes.

He took notes over a few more scriptures, vowing to read them during his week's devotional time.

When the time came for an altar call, a young man and an elderly woman came to accept Christ. Their walk down the aisle made Stanley smile for them. If they got in the Word and started getting to know some of the people at Warren Grove, they were in for a wonderful, new change.

After their confessions of faith, announcements were read, and then came the big moment.

Deacon Lewis called Stanley forward.

"Brothers and Sisters in Christ," he started.

Now that Stanley was facing the crowd and they were all seated, he could clearly spot Kim and Sabrina sitting next to one another. He smiled at them. They both discreetly waved at him. Stanley didn't think his heart could take any more.

That's when he saw Yolanda sitting on the right side of Kim. *She's here!* Stanley felt like running down the center aisle and grabbing his oldest child, telling her how much he loved her and how it meant the world to him that she had come. His eyes welled with tears.

"Brother Brown, is there anyone you'd like to recognize today? Anything you'd like to say to the congregation?"

Stanley hadn't heard anything else Deacon Lewis said. "Um... yes..." The speech had totally slipped his mind. "I just want to..." Stanley's voice caught in his throat. "I have three daughters here today. Kim, Sabrina, and Yolanda."

Deacon Lewis's face brightened with shock. "Wow, that's great."

"Yeah." Stanley swallowed. "And I have to admit that I didn't always do right by them. I didn't always do right by God. I've messed up a lot in my life, had a lot of regrets. But, like Pastor said today, for God so loved *the world*. That's *me*. I was *the world*. But God."

Warren Grove clapped in support of Stanley's words.

"To be honest with you, Deacon Lewis, I didn't really think you all would allow me to be a Deacon. Not after I told you the truth. But I know it was God who put me through that interview and made me come clean before Him and before my girls. And I'm grateful for that. This has already been a blessing to me, and I hope to be a blessing to my family. My spiritual family and my natural family."

"Amen!" Deacon Reed yelled out. "Bring your daughters on up here!"

With a few members seconding Deacon Reed's motion and the ushers clearing the way for his daughters, Kim, Sabrina, and Yolanda joined Stanley at the altar. With the church cheering them on, Kim approached first and hugged him. Then Sabrina. Then they stepped aside.

Finally, came Yolanda. Her eyes were filled with tears. Her face twisted in pain. She had made it to the altar but her feet weren't moving anymore.

Stanley took the steps needed to close the gap between them. He held out his arms, hoping beyond hope that Yolanda would receive him. *Please, God.*

Kim rubbed Yolanda's arm. "It's okay," she whispered to her sister.

With that, Yolanda collapsed into Stanley's chest and hugged him tighter than he had ever been hugged before. Her body trembled as she cried, and Stanley hugged her for all the past thirty years. For all the birthday parties he'd missed. All the Christmas gifts he'd never purchased, the times when she'd needed a father and hadn't known what to do. If one hug could have done it all, that one, that day was the one.

He kissed Yolanda's forehead. "I'm so sorry, Yolanda. I didn't do right before, but I gotcha now."

He pulled Kim and Sabrina into the tight circle. With the church still clapping, Stanley said only loud enough for his girls to hear. "Whatever it was in me that made me run away is gone now. Been replaced with the love of God. And I want to spend the rest of my life showing y'all Him through me. You hear?"

They all nodded. Even Kim was tearing up now.

Through his own tears, Stanley could see that several people in the audience were also shedding tears. His mother and Debbie were wiping their cheeks.

Stanley wondered how many people in the house had also grown up fatherless or even motherless. How many had run from their responsibilities as parents for whatever reason, and how many had carried the burden of single parenting. All he could do was hope that the scene they were witnessing would bless them somehow.

The ordination was nothing but a formality to Stanley by that point. Pastor and the Deacons said a few words, prayed over him, and gave him a big white Bible, which he wasn't sure he even wanted to use because the one He'd had for over a year now had all his sacred notes, his highlighting, and thoughts in the margins. Maybe he could use the big fancy one for the living room coffee table if he ever got his own house.

Until then, he'd probably keep it in the box.

Or maybe he'd give it to one of his grandchildren. Keep the legacy going.

When it was all said and done, Pastor gave the benediction and announced that there would be refreshments served in the fellowship hall.

Kim, Sabrina, and Yolanda rushed back to Stanley's side, and Debbie approached the trio with her phone camera handy.

"Stanley," she called to them, "y'all get together!"

And then she snapped the photograph of a lifetime, which Stanley would later share with total strangers in department stores and post on social media with the caption: Me and my beautiful daughters.

Discussion Questions

1. After Todderick's death, Stanley feels condemnation and wonders if he will ever truly escape his past. How do you handle condemnation? How do you deal with things you've done in the past that you'd rather not remember?

2. Jesse was angry that Yolanda had filed child support because he said it made him feel like a slave. What are your views about child support? Do you think it's something people do out of revenge or simply a practical matter? Is it a child's right? Do you think the system is unfair to men?

3. Yolanda was overcome with emotion upon seeing Stanley again, but she tucked her feelings away for the sake of her children? Should adults allow children to see them as vulnerable human beings? If so, where do we draw the line? If not, are we setting them up to feel like failures when they face inner turmoil?

4. Debbie doesn't want Stanley to spend time pursing her when he hasn't pursued relationships with his own children. Is this a stance that you think more women should take? Why or why not?

5. How does your church handle conflict amongst members?

6. Stanley says the reason people leave church is because of mess like the gossip Debbie heard. Would you agree? Why do you think there are so many people leaving church?

7. Yolanda doesn't deal with emotional stress because she's too busy raising her children. Can you relate? Is this a healthy way to deal with life? Realistically, what *can* she do?

8. Kim, Yolanda, and Sabrina have different ideas about Stanley's return. Which daughter can you relate to the most? Why?

9. Kim believes that Stanley's absence might have been God's protection from the life-damaging influence of Stanley's ways. Do you think this may be true?

10. Gwen purposely kept Jesse away from Yolanda and the kids to keep them from experiencing the heartache of a father who doesn't keep his word. Do you think Gwen was wrong?

11. Stanley's mother says that although she doesn't go to church, the Lord hears her prayers. What are your thoughts about the importance of attending a local church? Can a person grow in Christ without fellowship with believers? Does that fellowship have to look a certain way?

12. At the ordination, Deacon Reed nods at Stanley and Stanley says all is well between them. Is it easier for men (as opposed to women) to forgive and move on?

A Word from the Authors

T hank you so much for taking the time to read *Deacon Brown's Daughters*. It's a story that's near and dear to our hearts because both CaSandra and I (Michelle) have been affected by the issues our characters faced in this book. We understand Yolanda, Kim, and Sabrina as well as their moms. And I think everyone knows what it's like to have done something in the past that you're ashamed of.

It may not be as "big" as abandoning a child, but there's really no distinction between a little sin and a big sin in God's eyes. We have all fallen short at one time or another, and many of us have been the victims of somebody else's shortcomings.

We pray that this book will encourage disconnected parents to reach out to their children if they are still alive. Tragically, Stanley was never able to reach out to Todderick before his untimely death. If you still have the opportunity, take it. Perhaps by a letter, a card, a phone call. It may be uncomfortable at first, if your child is acting like Yolanda, but remember: It's not about you right now. Go *in there* and meet your child in that pit.

The strain between Stanley and his children's mothers is a very real conundrum as well. When the relationship ends badly, co-parenting can be extremely difficult. You can't make the other parent do right by the child, but whatever you do, please don't pass along any leftover bitterness. As in Yolanda's case, her emotions were simmering just beneath the surface, and her children were suffering the same way she had suffered because of Gwen's poisonous words (see the generational pattern there?).

Above all, we want our readers to have compassion upon one another, just as Christ has compassion for us. Who could stand if called to give account for every single wrong? Who can cast the first stone at Stanley? No one. And because of Christ, no eternally damning stones can be cast at us.

In His Love,
Michelle & CaSandra

Other books by CaSandra McLaughlin & Michelle Stimpson

All Available Online Now!

Not with the Church's Money

When the pastor of Lee Chapel passes away suddenly, his son, Willie Lee, Jr., is supposed to pick up the mantle. But "church" was never Willie Jr.'s forte...until his uncle Joseph convinces him that becoming the next pastor might prove beneficial financially.

Willie's mother, Ephesia, hopes that her son will be able to fill his father's shoes, but she has doubts. And Willie's Aunt Galatia has no problem voicing her opinions about Willie Jr.'s deficiencies. In fact, she hopes that her husband (Joseph) will soon be able to take over the job of shepherding the church.

Amidst this uncertainty, Willie's wife decides now would be a good time to leave, which means Willie Jr. must obtain and keep a job--something he hasn't ever really had to do. Will the pressures of making ends meet cause Willie Jr. to abuse his position and the church's money? Will he ever be able to live up to the prophecy his deceased father told? And will he learn his most valuable lessons before it's too late?

The Blended Blessings Series

Book 1: A New Beginning - Sometimes love doesn't work out the first time. Or the second. Now in her third marriage, Angelia is hoping for her happily-ever-after with Darren Holley. But soon after they move into their sprawling mini-mansion, Darren's new job as a high school football coach in a championship-hungry Texas town leaves Angelia feeling like a single mother to her two children as well as Darren's twin diva-daughters. Not to mention the drama from Darren's mother, who can't get over the fact that her son has married a woman with so much baggage.

When Angelia confides in a few ladies from the local church, their nice, sweet, holy-wife advice may prove too burdensome. Should Angelia cut her losses and get out before the ink settles on their marriage certificate, or will she finally learn the true meaning of perseverance as she and Darren attempt to blend two very different backgrounds in the face of adversity *and* nosy church folk?

Book 2: Through It All - Angelia Holley knows she'd never win a mother-of-the-year award. But was her example so bad that it drove her daughter, Amber, to repeat the pattern of teenage pregnancy? And why did Amber pick J.D. of all people to father her baby?

While Angelia is forming a bond with her stepdaughter, Skylar, twin sister Tyler isn't nearly as fond of the new "family" forming in the Holley household. When Tyler starts to act out, will Angelia be able to keep her mouth shut and let her husband and the girls' mother work this out?

And the baby of the family, Demarcus, suddenly wants to bond with his biological father. Should Angelia swallow her pride, overlook the years of lack of financial/emotional support, and allow

Demarcus to form a bond with the man who has never been there for him?

Join Angelia and Darren Holley as they continue with the growing pains of a blended family as they grow in their knowledge of the One who can help them through.

Book 3: Peace of Mind - Angelia Holley hopes that things in her blended family have made a turn for the better. She and her step-daughter, Tyler, are getting along better. Twin Skylar has fully recuperated from surgery and Angelia is even learning to embrace her new role as a much-too-young grandmother.

Just when Angelia gets a firm handle on life, up pops drama in the form of Javar—her oldest child's father, who had been imprisoned. Will Angelia be able to put her past life with her previous boo behind? Will Javar want a relationship with Amber and Dylan?

And then there's her meddling mother-in-law, Mother Holley. Will she ever accept Angelia as Darren's wife? Will Angelia's prayer group be able to help her stand on the word and her faith, trusting God to work it out?

Join Darren and Angelia in the final book of the Blended Blessings series to see if they will ever have peace of mind.

About the Authors

CaSandra McLaughlin was raised in Marshall, Texas. Growing up she wrote poems and loved to read books. She remembers being excited every time the book mobile came to her school. Reading always took her to another place, and often she would find herself rewriting an author's story. CaSandra wrote a play in high school for theatre that she received a superior rating on, and from there she aspired to be a writer.

CaSandra's a true believer that God has blessed us all with gifts and talents and it's up to us to tap into them to make our dreams come true. She's always dreamed of being on radio, TV and being an author. CaSandra currently works for a Gospel radio station and now she's an author. That lets her know that dreams come true—two down and one more to go. CaSandra wants people to read her work and feel encouraged, and it's her prayer that they read something that will change their lives and give them a ray of hope that things will be better. She's praying that God will continue to use her to write novels with several life lessons to help inspire the world.

CaSandra currently lives in Glenn Heights, Texas with her husband Richard and they have two amazing children. CaSandra loves God, her family, church, her friends, reading and Mexican food, in that order. Peace and blessings to all. Thanks for the love and support.
Visit CaSandra McLaughlin Online at
www.CaSandraMcLaughlin.com
http://www.facebook.com/casandra.marshallmclaughlin

Michelle Stimpson's works include the highly acclaimed *Boaz Brown*, *Divas of Damascus Road* (National Bestseller), and *Falling Into Grace*, which has been optioned for a movie. She has published several short stories for high school students through her educational publishing company at WeGottaRead.com.

Michelle serves in women's ministry at her home church, Oak Cliff Bible Fellowship. She regularly speaks at special events and writing workshops sponsored by churches, schools, book clubs, and educational organizations.

The Stimpsons are proud parents of two young adults, grandparents of one super-sweet granddaughter, and the owners of one Cocker Spaniel, Mimi, who loves to watch televangelists.

Visit Michelle online:
www.MichelleStimpson.com
https://www.facebook.com/MichelleStimpsonWrites

Made in the USA
Lexington, KY
14 August 2017